Magical Mystery Paws

KU-238-206

MAGICAL MYSTERY PAWS

The No. 2 **FELINE** Detective Agency

MANDY MORTON

First published in 2018 by Farrago,
an imprint of Prelude Books Ltd
13 Carrington Road, Richmond, TW10 5AA, United Kingdom

www.farragobooks.com

ISBN: 978-1-78842-098-3

*In memory of Boobah and Kitty O'Shea,
and always Hettie and Tilly*

Chapter One

The town had been basking in warm summer sunshine since the beginning of May. A long, cold winter had made way for a short spring, before the grey clouds parted to reveal day after day of deep blue skies, hot pavements and a general air of sleepy contentment as cats slept out on doorsteps and found cool shady areas in their gardens.

The No. 2 Feline Detective Agency, run by Hettie Bagshot and her friend Tilly Jenkins, had all but closed for the season. After a busy winter of burglaries, missing kittens and a spate of serial shoplifting, all had gone quiet – which, of course, was the way Hettie liked it. Summer was for dreaming in the sunshine and casting all cares away, but even Hettie Bagshot could get bored and, as she shuffled her deckchair out of the shadow of her friend Bruiser's shed, there was much grumbling. 'The thing is,' she began, 'if we'd known it was going to be hot all summer, we could have taken one of those beach hut things on the sands at Southwool!'

'Ooh, that would have been lovely,' said Tilly, putting her latest Polly Hodge thriller down for long enough to consider Hettie's outburst, and sensing that there was more to come.

'And another thing…' Hettie continued, as Tilly applied more cream to her sunburnt ears. 'If we *did* want to do something exciting, it's too hot anyway. Even Miss Scarlet's petrol is evaporating in the heat and Bruiser wouldn't be seen dead in his leathers in these temperatures.' Hettie nodded towards the shed that their friend Bruiser shared with Miss Scarlet, a rather fine bright red motorbike and sidecar which was the chosen mode of transport for their detective business.

Bruiser had strayed back into Hettie's life one cold snowy morning after years tramping the highways and sleeping under the stars – but old bones felt the cold, and he had been instantly accepted by her landladies, Betty and Beryl Butter. He was now a permanent fixture in all their lives as a lad about the yard and a key member of the No. 2 FDA, as the business was affectionately known.

'Well, maybe we should make an effort to have a nice day out,' suggested Tilly, trying to head off Hettie's bad temper. 'We could get Betty to make up a packed lunch and have a picnic in a field or something, or even go and sit by the river.'

Tilly had clearly said the wrong thing: far from calming the waters, she had released a tirade that had been simmering since Hettie finished her second bacon bap at breakfast. 'In a bloody field! Why on earth would we want to do that? We'd be sharing with wasps, cowpats, grass snakes, and assorted flora and fauna – all waiting to bring on a bout of sneezing. Then there's the hike with the deckchairs, rugs, bottles of fiery ginger beer and – in your case – three different sorts of sun cream.' Tilly was about to protest, but Hettie pushed on as Bruiser emerged from his shed, rubbing his eyes and wondering what the noise was about. 'And might I point out that last time we had a day by the river, it was dramatically cut short by you falling off the back of Poppa's narrowboat and getting tangled in a moorhen's nest.'

'I was reading *The Wind in the Willows* at the time,' said Tilly, offering a weak defence.

The rattle of a tea tray proved a welcome distraction as Betty Butter made her way down the garden. 'Me and sister are closing up for the day. We're off to the garden centre because it's too hot to work in the bakery, so I've brought a few leftovers from the lunchtime rush. There's salmon turnovers, cheese pasties, a couple of ham rolls and a selection of cream cakes, but you'll have to be quick, as they're sliding off the plates in this heat.'

Betty and Beryl Butter had thrown caution to the wind and left their native Lancashire and moved South to buy up the town's old run-down bakery with a small legacy left to them by their mother. In a matter of months, the two large white cats were running a flourishing business, and it wasn't long before their pies and pastries gained legendary status. Their hearts were as warm as their ovens: when Hettie was made homeless, they offered her the small room at the back of their bakery, then allowed the same safe harbour for Tilly, as her arthritic paws could no longer stand harsh winters. The two long-haired tabby cats had settled into their accommodation in style: Tilly was the homemaker and Hettie the so-called brains of the outfit. It was Tilly's love of the detective novel that had first given her friend the idea for their current occupation, and now – several high-profile cases down the line – the No. 2 Feline Detective Agency could be deemed a moderate success.

In an uncharacteristic burst of energy, Hettie struggled from her deckchair and relieved Betty of the tray, bringing it to rest on the garden bench outside Bruiser's shed, which seemed to be the only place offering any shade. Showing their delight at Betty's gifts, Hettie, Tilly and Bruiser made short work of the cream cakes and, after much licking and cleaning of whiskers, they set about the savouries with equal enthusiasm.

Betty had barely returned to the bakery when yet another visitor sidled down the garden path. 'Wotcha,' said Poppa. 'I thought I'd find you taking in some rays. Too hot for anything else, really, unless you all fancy an adventure?'

The black-and-white cat threw himself onto a lush patch of lawn and Tilly handed him the last of the ham rolls. Poppa Phene was the town's plumber – and a very fine one at that – but he had been a friend to Hettie for more years than either of them could remember, mostly due to the haze of catnip they had lived through during Hettie's professional music career, when Poppa was her roadie and constant companion. When Hettie had finally decided to hang up her guitar, Poppa had started a lucrative plumbing business from his houseboat on the river and supplied an extra pair of paws, when required, to his friend's detective business.

'What do you mean by an adventure?' asked Hettie, scraping some patisserie cream out of her fur.

Poppa poked the final piece of ham roll into his mouth and chewed slowly, as if thinking of a good place to start. Tilly moved forward on her deckchair, while Bruiser pulled up an upturned bucket and settled himself down between her and Hettie. Seeing that his audience was waiting patiently, Poppa began. 'Well, I got meself in a bit of a fix, really. I've been doin' some running round for Patty Sniff lately. She's been in Tabby Road, recording her latest album with her new band, The Cheese Triangles.'

Tilly stifled a giggle, as Poppa continued. 'Anyway, as you probably know, Patty is blind. That's why she's called Patty Sniff – her real name is Fiona Foxglove and she's been off the road for a bit on account of her creative juices dryin' up. She was quite something in her bin bag days, but there doesn't seem to be much interest in cat punk anymore.'

'You mean she can't get any gigs,' interrupted Hettie.

'Yup, that's about the size of it. This new album is make or break for her, but she's got to tour it or she's dead in the water. That's where I come in. I've put some dates together but the venues wouldn't take her on her own, so I've had to add a few acts to bulk things out a bit – like a touring party, really. We're calling it the Summer of Fluff Tour.'

Tilly was now on the very edge of her seat with excitement, and pre-empted Hettie by jumping in with both front paws. 'And you'd like us to help with the tour?'

'Well, let's just put it this way: I have a number of senior tour personnel to engage, and I thought this would be right up your street.'

Tilly clapped her paws together and danced round her deckchair as Hettie aired a cautious note. 'What sort of things would you need us to do?'

'I need a bus driver, so that would be good for Bruiser. I've hired a single-decker charabanc from Psycho Derek. He's doing the warm-up bit on tour, calling himself

Magical Mystery Paws... some sort of illusionist. I had to take him on because he comes with the bus. Then I'll need costume and backstage production, and I thought Tilly might be good at that – a steady pair of paws is just what's needed.'

Tilly could hardly contain herself. In spite of the heat, she felt the urge to skip round the Butters' lawn, kicking up a dust storm as she went. Bruiser looked pleased and was keen to find out more, but Hettie needed further convincing. 'So what have you got in mind for me?' she asked.

'The top job, of course,' responded Poppa, knowing that an ego massage was the only way to go with his old friend. 'Let's face it,' he continued, 'no one knows the road like you do. All those tours we did, all those scrapes we got in and out of: breakdowns, weather, power cuts – we had the lot. I'll want to put you in charge of the whole thing. Who else could do the job?'

Hettie suddenly felt flooded with a new sense of purpose. Her music days had brought her great joy. She had been reasonably successful with her band and she sometimes missed the call of the open road, but there was so much more to be discussed before she was ready to nail her colours to the Summer of Fluff mast. 'So we've got Patty Sniff and The Cheese Triangles... I'm assuming there are three of them besides Patty?' Poppa nodded. 'Then we've got Psycho Derek doing magic tricks, parading himself as Magical Mystery Paws. Does he have an assistant?'

'Belisha Beacon,' offered Poppa. 'She works in the café at Tabby Road Studios when she's not on crossing patrol, but Derek's taken a fancy to her so she's coming along for the ride.'

'So we've got six performers to look after?' said Hettie. 'Well, that shouldn't be too bad.'

'Ah,' said Poppa, 'then there's the Irish dance troupe.'

'The what?' exclaimed Hettie.

'Kitty O'Shea's Irish dancers, all the way from Donegal. There's six of them, plus Boobah, their French dance mistress. They're straight from a season of Riverdance. There used to be seven, but one of them drowned in the grand finale.'

Pausing slightly to digest Poppa's remarks, and sharing a concerned look with Tilly and Bruiser, Hettie thought it best to stay positive. She launched into a selection of more practical matters. 'When does the tour start? How many dates are there? And is there any money involved?'

Poppa decided to tackle the sticky issue first. 'Money could be a bit of a sod – as no one's got any – but if the venues pay up, we should be able to have a bit of a share-out at the end. I've got six dates confirmed, with two in the pipeline, and the tour starts on Monday at West Grunting Pavilion. We're doing Southwool Pier as the last gig, so at least that one is close to home.'

'Monday?' shouted Hettie, as if everyone around her was deaf. 'But today is Thursday! That's only four days to get ready.'

'Yup,' responded Poppa, 'spot on! But I've booked the Methodist Hall in Cheapcuts Lane for tomorrow to have a bit of a rehearsal, check out the gear and iron out any wrinkles. You should come along and meet everyone.'

The first black cloud of the summer lurched across the sun, throwing the garden into shadow, and Hettie felt a chill pass through her. Premonition or not, she knew in her heart that the Summer of Fluff Tour was doomed before it had begun, and tomorrow would confirm her worst fears.

Chapter Two

Cheapcuts Lane was at the bottom of the High Street and, whenever Hettie could spare her from her detective duties, Tilly spent many a happy hour there, in her friend Jessie's charity shop. Jessie's late benefactor, Miss Lambert, had given her a home and had also taken Tilly in on winter nights, feeding her and letting her curl up by the fire. Tilly and Jessie had become firm friends, sharing a love of brightly coloured clothes. Tilly had a particular passion for knitted cardigans so Jessie made sure that there was plenty of stock to choose from in exchange for a couple of hours' help behind the counter, from time to time. The charity shop was a huge success. No one could quite remember which charity it honoured, but the low prices for clothes and other essentials served the community in the best of ways, and Jessie's idea of turning Miss Lambert's front room into a shop had given her the security she needed to pursue her flair for make-do-and-mend.

When Hettie, Tilly and Bruiser turned into Cheapcuts Lane, Jessie was completing a beach scene in her window, featuring sun hats, swimsuits, and a selection of colourfully painted kitten-sized buckets and spades. Hettie glanced across the road towards the Methodist Hall, noting that the padlock was still on the door. There was no sign of Poppa's Transit van or Psycho Derek's bus; clearly, the rehearsal was a little late in starting, which gave them a good excuse to plunder Jessie's shop for new stock while they waited for the tour party to arrive.

'Well,' said Jessie, hurling her door open in an enthusiastic welcome, 'not just one detective but all three of you! It must be a big case, and it's not even ten o'clock. Come on – what gives? And I need all the details. I'll pop the kettle on and check out the state of the biscuit tin.' She disappeared through a red beaded curtain at the back of the shop, leaving Hettie, Tilly and Bruiser to browse.

Tilly immediately leapt on a tangerine, purple and red poncho, slipping it over her head and parading herself in front of a large mirror, satisfied that the item was just what she was looking for. Bruiser settled himself in a corner, happy to flick through back copies of *Biker's Monthly*, and Hettie was eyeing up the bric-a-brac, when a spectacle unfolding at the Methodist Hall drew her to the window. To say that the primary colours of Psycho Derek's bus were blue and yellow would be to oversimplify the flowers, birds, stars, frenetic swirls and various peace symbols which were emblazoned on the bodywork. Hettie could just about pick out the words 'Summer of Fluff Tour', but the letters struggled to be seen amid a hotchpotch of pop-art ramblings. The decorative aspect of the bus was certainly making quite a statement in Cheapcuts Lane, but it was the fact that it was being pushed into the car park of the Methodist Hall that concerned Hettie. 'Just come and look at this – it's like a bad film from the sixties!' She was joined at the window by Tilly and Bruiser, as Jessie emerged from the back of the shop with four steaming mugs of tea and a pile of sticky flapjacks.

'Blimey!' said Bruiser. 'Am I s'posed to drive that? And why are all those weird cats pushin' it?'

'I think you'll find that those weird cats are the touring party,' said Hettie. 'I assume that the cat steering it and wearing all those beads round his neck is Psycho Derek. The ones wearing ballet shoes and green tabards must be the Irish dance troupe, and that cat standing in the middle of the road looking bewildered is definitely Patty Sniff.'

'So it is!' squealed Jessie. 'I remember seeing her at The Fish Scaler's Arms back in the day. Closed the place down, she did – her three-night stand turned into twenty minutes of spitting and she was out on her safety-pinned ear. I don't think any of us were ready for her new-wave punk antics, but just look at her now! She looks like something Halloween rejected, and all those long grey dreadlocks aren't exactly of the moment. Why is she here?'

Hettie had a mouth full of flapjack, so it was left to Tilly to explain the finer details of Poppa's tour. The bus finally settled across three parking spaces and the tour party clambered back on board, exhausted and completely forgetting about Patty Sniff, who spent some time clawing at the back of the bus to find the door. Seconds later, Poppa's van arrived. With an ever-hopeful spring in his step, he decanted the contents of the tour bus – including a large black-and-white cat in a wheelchair, who seemed to be issuing orders to anyone who would listen – into the Methodist Hall.

'We could just go home now and forget the whole thing,' said Hettie, draining her mug. 'I haven't seen anything I like the look of going into that hall. We're in for trouble all the way if we take that lot on.'

'Yes, I think you're scuppered this time,' agreed Jessie, digging Hettie in the ribs. 'Look who's on her way over.'

Patty Sniff was weaving a circuitous route across the street, as several delivery vans and a startled cyclist manoeuvred around her. On reaching the pavement, her final encounter with a mother and double buggy full of kittens was nearly her undoing, but Jessie averted what promised to be an unseemly altercation. Acting swiftly, she hooked the blind singer into her shop and out of harm's way.

'Yeah, right, that's really cool of you,' said Patty to no one in particular, realising that she'd reached some form of safe harbour. 'Just point me in the direction of the action and I'll be fine. Should have brought me stick, but it's just another hassle in a long line of hassles. I've been at the end of me string lately, what with having to get the album out. Laying down the tracks was a nightmare, and so was breaking in a new band. I'm a bit short on space in me head, if you know what I mean.'

They had absolutely no idea what Patty meant, although the words 'lost cause' entered Hettie's head. Poppa had emerged from the Methodist Hall and was looking underneath the bus, as if he'd lost something; clearly, it was time to steer Patty Sniff towards the action. Jessie collected the mugs, wrapped up Tilly's poncho, refusing to take any money for it, and waved her friends off with a good-luck salute, which they were certainly going to need. Hettie guided Patty back across the street into the safe and grateful paws of Poppa, who thought he'd lost his star turn. Hettie and Tilly left Bruiser staring into the silent bus engine, scratching his head, and followed Poppa and Patty into the Methodist Hall, where hell had broken loose in the shape of Boobah, the wheelchaired dancing mistress.

Chapter Three

The town's Methodist Hall had stood as a solid symbol of community activities for many years, welcoming scout and guide troops, bingo and whisker drives, the Friendship Club, salsa and cat aerobics classes, hot yoga sessions, and the occasional disco – but its creaking floorboards had never been subjected to the violent thumping of Boobah's silver-topped cane as she beat time and the ankles of her dance troupe in equal measure.

Poppa delivered Patty Sniff to the stage-end of the hall to await the arrival of her band, leaving the floor area free for Kitty O'Shea's Irish dance troupe to be put through their paces by the formidable Miss Boobah. No one knew quite how long she'd been confined to her wheelchair, or why; it was one of those questions that never seemed to have been asked. Kitty had met the dance mistress at the Irish Step Dance Championships several years before, and Boobah quickly attached herself to the ensemble, making herself irreplaceable in a very short space of time. Despite regarding herself as French, Boobah had a definite Russian brusqueness to her manner, which frightened the dancers into believing that violence would be done if they didn't meet her high standards; consequently, Kitty's company danced off with every trophy and accolade available from the moment that Boobah wheeled her chair into the middle of them. The troupe had just completed a six-week run at the Hammersniff Odeon, which ended in tragedy when Cathal O'Crumb was washed from the stage by a tidal wave caused by an overly enthusiastic stagehand who forgot to turn the tap off during the final moments of Riverdance. Cathal lingered until the following Tuesday, but finally succumbed to pneumonia, and Kitty – being fairly astute with her finances – decided not to replace him in order to have more of the spoils to share out. She also pocketed a sizeable sum of compensation from the Odeon, which had made its way across the Irish Sea and now resided under Kitty's mattress in her cottage overlooking Dingle Bay.

Hettie and Tilly stared in amazement as the dancers twisted themselves up onto their points, bobbing up and down in perfect time to the pounding rhythm of Boobah's cane. 'And one and two, step and hop, tip step, tip step, treble hop, back. Come on, Mr Cormac, keep up! And Moya – take that catnip lozenge out of your mouth before you choke yourself. This vill not do! You are all so sluggish. Tarmac! Straighten your arms – you nearly took Aisling's eye out – and get those claws clipped before the tour starts. Enya, you seem to be playing too slowly. We don't want to be treated to your ethereal nonsense – the jig must be strident and energetic!' Boobah brought her cane down with a crash onto the slight but very beautiful cat's keyboard, and Enya's large brown eyes filled with two equally large tears. Kitty left the line of dancers to give Enya a hug, as Boobah generously gave the cats a two-minute break.

Looking around the hall, Hettie spotted the cat she assumed to be Psycho Derek. With him was a middle-aged, fluffy grey-haired cat, who was more than a little overweight and bursting out of an unseasonal shiny red Mary Quaint mac. She'd finished off her look with a pair of high white-plastic boots and considerably too much eye make-up, which gave her the look of a panda. Belisha Beacon had started out as a crossing attendant outside the now famous Tabby Road Recording Studios, where she had helped many a well-known artist across the busy street. As a perk, she had taken her tea break in the studio's small basement café in the vain hope of being talent-spotted whilst collecting autographs to sell on to fans. As luck would have it, she was indeed spotted by the café manager, who invited her to butter baps three times a week during the lunchtime rush. Belisha managed to combine her crossing duties with bap buttering for several months, until there was a misunderstanding on the crossing involving a laundry van and several members of a high-profile group, who remain nameless due to the ongoing court case. Psycho Derek was passing in his bus and offered assistance to Belisha, who had caught her lollipop stick under one of the front wheels of the laundry van. Derek scooped her off the crossing and onto his bus, where they had been living together ever since.

Glancing from one side of the hall to the other, and taking in the talent – or lack of it – Hettie's instinct was to run for the door while she still could, dragging Tilly with her, but Poppa joined them just in time to head off her departure. 'I'll 'ave to go and fetch The Cheese Triangles,' he said. 'Their Reliant Robin's broken down on the

Southwool Road. If you could keep an eye on Patty for me that would be great – she's a bit disorientated. She's got her knitting, so she should be fine till I get back. And go to say hello to Derek and Belisha – looks like he's checking out some tricks.' Poppa nodded in the direction of the panda in the red mac and left before Hettie could argue.

'I wonder how Bruiser is getting on with the bus?' said Tilly brightly, as Boobah resumed her reign of terror with the Irish dancers. 'Just think: if he can't fix it, we won't be able to go on tour.'

Hettie was about to respond when Bruiser made his way into the hall, covered in grease and carrying what looked like a large black spider. 'It's the distributor, I think – filthy. And them spark plugs 'ave seen better days. Needs a service and an oil change, then she'll go like a good 'un. I s'pose I'd better 'ave a word with Derek, as it's his bus.'

Hettie nodded as a crash came from the stage. It appeared that Patty Sniff was on the move and had become tangled up in a bag of microphone stands. Tilly leapt to her aid, leaving Hettie and Bruiser to discuss the finer points of vehicle maintenance with Psycho Derek.

'Can I help, Miss Sniff?' offered Tilly, disentangling the singer from the microphone stands. 'I'm Tilly Jenkins, and I'm in charge of costumes and backstage.'

'Yeah, right. As you can see, I can't. I dropped me knitting needle, and it's just too far out for me to deal with right now. Not entirely sure about the colours anyway. I always used to knit on tour. Sometimes I'd sit at the back of the stage while the band did their stuff. You know, drum solos and all that. I knitted a whole scarf once during a lead guitar break. I think that was the night the audience went home four hours before we did, but I can't be sure of anything really.'

Tilly gently guided the punk star back to her chair, grabbing the stray needle on the way. Once Patty was safely seated again, Tilly gathered up the knitting, which resembled nothing she'd ever seen before. The shapeless bundle of wool looked like a care home for moths. Armholes and cuffs blended in with long stretches of stocking stitch, which seemed to be unpicking itself before Tilly's eyes. Patty Sniff's knitting was a disaster area and Tilly suddenly felt very sad for the singer, who appeared to be trapped in her own living nightmare. 'Is there anything I can get you, Miss Sniff, while you wait for your band? Poppa has gone to fetch them, and they shouldn't be too long.'

'That's really kind, but I think I'll just sit here and run through me lyrics. I could murder a catnip roll-up, but I've left me tin on the bus so I'll 'ave one later. And you can call me Patty. Miss Sniff sounds like an old schoolteacher who used to beat me up for not lookin' at the blackboard – bit pointless in my case, but she liked to 'ave a go at me whenever she could. Fascist Scum – that was her name. Or was it Vera Dread? No, I think Vera did the support on me Slash and Burn tour.'

Tilly left the singer on the stage, mumbling her way through her first set of songs. She joined Hettie and Bruiser, who seemed to be having a rather heated conversation with Psycho Derek, aided and abetted by Belisha Beacon. 'Look matey,' said Bruiser. 'That bus is goin' nowhere without a service – unless you can magic a set of new sparks and some oil from somewhere.'

''E could magic them if 'e wanted to,' chimed in Belisha. 'I bet 'e could make you disappear, too, if 'e wanted. You don't seem to realise that you're talking to *the* Magical Mystery Paws 'imself, master of illusion.'

It was Hettie's turn to offer some advice, as only she could. 'Well, Miss Beacon, if Derek here is so good at magic, I suggest that he goes and fires up the engine on that bus out there to prove to us all that the vehicle is capable of doing the tour. Or he could let my good friend Bruiser here sort the problem out with his magic wand instead.'

Belisha was about to offer another penny's worth of vitriol when Derek conceded by shaking Bruiser's paw and reluctantly pulling a collection of coins out of his waistcoat pocket. 'I don't reckon my magic will stretch to mechanics. All I can say is that she was runnin' fine when I bought her, and I only really wanted something to practise me art on, see. I tell you what – here's a few bob towards the stuff you need. Poppa will have to cough up the rest.'

Belisha was crushed by the happy outcome, having appointed herself as Psycho Derek's protector. Bruiser sidled off in the direction of Lazarus Hambone's yard to pick up the oil and spark plugs he needed, while Hettie and Tilly settled themselves down to watch Derek and Belisha rehearse their magic tricks. It soon became very clear that Psycho Derek hadn't got a magical bone in his body, and teaming up with Belisha Beacon only made his lack of talent more visible. Hettie was shocked when Derek proceeded to break the seal on a new box of magic tricks: coloured balls, egg cups, bits of string, a set of rings, a pack of cards, and an assortment of dice and thimbles all came tumbling out onto the floor. Derek pounced on the magic wand that was the last thing out of the box, twisting and twirling it in his paws, as Belisha began to read from the book of instructions.

Tilly's eyes grew wide with excitement, as Derek hit first the coloured balls and then the rings with his magic wand, standing back to take a bow to an imaginary audience – but nothing had changed: the coloured balls and set of rings remained in exactly the same state as before. Undaunted, Derek took up the cards, offering them to Tilly to choose one. 'Now take a long look at that card and tell me what it is,' he said.

'It's the three of diamonds,' Tilly replied.

'Excellent,' said Derek. 'Now, put the card back in the pack and tap the pack with your paw.'

Tilly did as she was told, waiting for the trick. Derek stared at the cards, struck them with his magic wand and then proceeded to sort through the pack until he came to the three of diamonds. He pulled it out with a flourish, which sent the rest of the cards skidding across the floor, and paraded it in front of Tilly's nose. 'There you are! Your card: the three of diamonds!'

Hettie was having problems digesting what she had just seen with her own eyes. The incompetence of the magician before her was so bad that it was almost brilliant. Tilly was less impressed, and wasted no time in saying so. 'But I told you my card was the three of diamonds,' she protested, 'which means it wasn't magic at all.'

Derek was suddenly busy collecting the cards from the floor, leaving Belisha to stand his corner. 'I can see you're one of those cats who likes to pick faults where there ain't none. Your trouble is you just don't believe in magic – and if you don't believe in magic then magic don't 'appen. You'll soon change your tune when you see Derek's disappearing box! He's famous for that!'

Derek looked more than a little confused by Belisha's outburst. He had no recollection of ever doing a trick with a disappearing box; in fact, he had little memory of succeeding with any trick at all, but he had bluffed his way through life, aspiring to dizzy heights which he would never reach. In Psycho Derek's world, anything and everything was possible; since teaming up with Belisha, his belief in himself had magnified – or spiralled out of control.

Chapter Four

Hettie was cross, and even Tilly – who always tried to look on the bright side – had entered into a slough of despond. Poppa's tour was a disaster. The magician had no magic in him and – with the exception of Lavender Stamp, the town's postmistress – his assistant was the most irritating cat that Hettie had ever met. Kitty O'Shea's Irish dancers were obviously competent, but more than a little out of place. And as for Patty Sniff, Hettie was of the opinion that things could only get worse once The Cheese Triangles arrived. The fact that the all-female backing band drove a Reliant Robin had done little to boost her confidence in them, and she was finding it hard to believe that Patty could handle anything more than a tuna sandwich. As soon as the thought of a sandwich popped into her head, Hettie realised that there was one very pressing matter to be dealt with. 'Come on,' she said, steering Tilly towards the door. 'Let's get out of here. I'll treat you to a poke of chips and some batter scraps from Elsie Haddock's.'

'But what about Patty?' protested Tilly. 'She can't be left on her own in a strange place.'

'I think Patty Sniff lives in a strange place most of the time,' mumbled Hettie. 'Poppa should be back any minute, and we could ask Kitty O'Shea to keep an eye on her.'

Tilly glanced across the hall to the clutch of dancers, who seemed to be huddled in a group hug around Boobah and her wheelchair. 'I think they're having some sort of strategy meeting,' she observed.

'The only bloody strategy needed here is to get the hell out while we still can!' replied Hettie, striding towards the door and bumping into The Cheese Triangles as Poppa ushered them in.

'How's it goin'?' asked Poppa, seeing the look of thunder on Hettie's face and noting that her long-haired tabby hackles were bristling.

Hettie couldn't resist a sarcastic reply, even though Poppa was one of her oldest and best friends. 'The fact is, it's not going at all. Or, to be more precise, we aren't going on this tour unless you can find some talent to entertain an audience without them demanding their money back!'

Poppa was used to Hettie's outbursts and decided to paper over the cracks by introducing The Cheese Triangles. 'Talent is just what we've got! Allow me to introduce Suzi Quake, Alice Slap and Deirdre Nightshade – known collectively as the one and only Cheese Triangles.'

Hettie's day got a whole lot worse as she set eyes on three very thin, short-haired cats, dressed in varying amounts of black plastic and sporting extreme examples of body piercing. Hettie had little doubt that they were the one and only; Patty Sniff suddenly became quite normal by comparison with these harpies, who paraded up and down like the original brides of Dracula.

Alice, Deirdre and Suzi skipped off to the stage to be reunited with Patty, and Poppa attempted to mend some broken fences. 'I know it's a bit of a rabble so far,' he said to Hettie, 'but Patty's a real star. Wait till I get the gear set up, then you'll see what they can do.'

'All right, but not on an empty stomach. We'll be back in an hour. I'm not holding out any great hope for the future of this tour, though.'

Hettie and Tilly emerged into the sunshine and headed for the High Street. As always, there was a queue at Elsie Haddock's fish and chip shop. Elsie was a one-cat band and ran her food outlet with regimented precision. Her weekday lunchtime queues stretched all the way to Hilda Dabbit's dry cleaners, and her customers knew that once the allotted cod and haddock had run out, the frying would cease immediately and Elsie would put her feet up in her conservatory until the evening session. Hettie and Tilly joined the queue, salivating as the smell of fried fish engulfed their nostrils.

As the customers moved slowly forward, Hettie decided to reflect on her touring days. Tilly loved it when her friend was in the right frame of mind to recall some of her adventures. She rarely talked about her music, but now and again Tilly sensed her extreme sadness at having had to give it up. 'The trouble is,' Hettie began, 'punk did for us. One minute everyone wanted flower-power folk rock, and the next no one would pay to put good music on anymore. The new wave lot turned up at gigs on the bus, couldn't tune their guitars, shouted abuse at the audience, pogoed and spat for an hour, smashed up the venue and went back home on the bus. And they didn't mind playing for free – not that anyone would ever offer to pay them, but the young cats couldn't get enough of them. They filled the venues night after night, paying to be part of what they called the anti-establishment. What they didn't realise was that our music had been fighting the same things in a much more peaceful way. We were anti-war, but they seemed to be anti-everything. They destroyed the established music scene. We couldn't afford to stay on the road and all the gigs dried up.'

'That's a very sad story,' said Tilly. 'Why do you think Patty is trying to make a comeback? The nice music is being played again, so she's going to be a bit out of date if she's doing punk stuff.'

'I dread to think what she's going to do,' said Hettie. 'She was one of the better ones as far as I remember. I think she could actually sing, but I don't hold out much hope for her with The Cheese Triangles… speaking of food, we're next!'

Hettie and Tilly found a quiet, shady spot in the grave-yard of St Kipper's to eat their chips and batter bits. With every mouthful, Hettie's mood improved. She was fond of graveyards and the town's central church boasted a rather fine one. It wasn't the religious aspect of St Kipper's that drew Hettie in, and the town's dead had no special attrac-tion, but the names carved into the army of headstones had inspired her in her songwriting days. Names were important: they could tell stories on their own, and she had no hesitation in borrowing them once their owners had moved on. These days, some of the names resonated with both Hettie and Tilly – cats who had left the earth prematurely and been part of some of the high-profile murder cases that had landed on their desk at the No. 2 Feline Detective Agency. Teezle Makepeace and Mavis Spitforce now rested under nearby trees, no longer burdened by the cares of everyday life; although that made them sad, Hettie and Tilly were proud of the fact that – thanks to them – their murderers were tucked away beyond the consecrated ground, unrecognised by any headstone, and as if they had never been. Justice had been served.

Finishing up the last few crispy bits and licking her paws, Hettie pulled herself up. 'Come on. Let's try to make some sense of the Summer of Fluff Tour. I owe it to Poppa to help out with this one and it might even be fun.'

Tilly was pleased that Hettie had brightened up. Food nearly always did the trick, and the prospect of a road trip, whatever it threw at them, was something to look forward to during these long, hot summer days. By the time they reached the Methodist Hall, the mood inside had changed dramatically. The stage was alive with strobe lighting and dry ice, as Patty Sniff emerged out of the swirling smoke to deliver a hell-raising anthem of protest and not-so-social comment – all to the throbbing beat of Alice Slap's drums, Suzi Quake's thundering bass lines and Deirdre Nightshade's piercing lead guitar, which punctuated Patty's vocals with sharp discords and gave the sound a vital edge. The other performers stared in amazement at the on-stage spectacle.

Hettie crossed to the centre of the hall, where Poppa was mixing the sound on an old, battered mixing desk. 'I recognise that desk!' she shouted over a rather brash guitar solo, which Deirdre appeared to be playing with her teeth. 'I didn't realise you'd kept it. Those faders did a few tours for us!'

Poppa smiled as Patty brought the current song to a crashing end by kicking one of Alice's cymbal stands over – for dramatic effect, or perhaps by mistake. 'I couldn't face getting rid of all the gear when you came off the road,' he said, switching off the strobes. 'The old stuff's the best. Even the multicore works, and the mikes and stands are all in good nick.'

Hettie stared wistfully at the stage set-up, noting that Patty was using her old vocal mike. 'They are very good,' she conceded. 'I can see why you were so keen to do the tour. If you're not careful, we might actually make some money – as long as Derek and his assistant only do a short warm-up, and Kitty O'Shea's lot take care of the interval.'

Poppa beamed, pleased to have Hettie on side at last. The Cheese Triangles pounded out another of Patty's latest efforts and Tilly, who had placed herself in front of the stage for the full effect, was transfixed by the singer. Patty moved in and out of her vocals as if her blindness didn't exist, crouching and leaping, note-perfect and leaving no one watching in any doubt that the stage was her comfort zone. In the few feet of space between her and her microphone stand, she was a star.

There were many comings and goings during the afternoon. Dorcas Ink arrived with the tour posters that Poppa had ordered. Dorcas was a little hard of hearing, and because she took instructions for her posters over the phone, there would sometimes be a knock-on effect with the finished product. The summer before, she had produced posters for the town's first literary event, which actually announced a 'Littertray Festival'; needless to say, those posters had become very collectable. Poppa had gone into the printing works in person to avoid a repeat performance and had spelt everything out for Dorcas. To his relief, the posters were fine: even the odd ink smudge was in keeping with the punk aspect of the tour, and the lurid colours set off the Summer of Fluff Tour to perfection. Derek was a little sulky about his billing at the bottom of the line-up, but Belisha placated him by pointing out that the headliners had more to prove and that Magical Mystery Paws was going to be a sensation. Hettie didn't doubt it, and almost said so in her best sarcastic voice.

Later that afternoon, after procuring almost-new spark plugs and oil from Lazarus Hambone for a very good price, Bruiser announced triumphantly that the bus was mobile again. He treated the ensemble to a quick trip up and down Cheapcuts Lane, and left them to choose their seats for the tour, which would double as their overnight accommodation. Derek and Belisha, who lived on the bus already, had a comfortable section of their own at the back, offering home comforts such as proper beds, a coffee table, curtains and a small cupboard where they kept treats for their midnight feasts. Belisha had made sure that there would be no misunderstandings from fellow travellers by placing a notice on the curtain, announcing that everything beyond that point was 'PRIVIT'.

Boobah, of course, had special needs for herself and her wheelchair, and with this in mind, Bruiser had borrowed a ramp from Lazarus to save bumping the dance mistress up and down the steps of the bus. She had chosen a double seat at the very front, with extra leg room and the opportunity to give helpful advice to Bruiser on his driving. Kitty and her dancers fell into the seats behind Boobah, making sure that the two male cats, Cormac and Tarmac, were segregated from Enya and Aisling. Kitty had promised the girls' mothers back in Donegal that she would look after their moral welfare, while secretly adopting the mantra of 'what goes on tour, stays on tour'.

There was a brief dispute between The Cheese Triangles and Poppa over the Reliant Robin: the band wanted to take their three-wheeler with them, but Poppa was of the opinion that the not-so-reliant vehicle was an extra complication which he could do without. Reluctantly – with bad grace and a load of expletives that Tilly had certainly never heard before – Alice, Deirdre and Suzi took up three double seats behind the dance troupe.

Hettie had already pointed out that the other side of the bus should be reserved for administration and management, and had saved six double seats for herself, Tilly, Bruiser and Poppa. It was Tilly who pointed out that there was no allocation for Patty; while the rest of the party was joyriding up and down Cheapcuts Lane, the star of the tour was still patting and sniffing to find her way down from the stage in the Methodist Hall, and had missed out on choosing her seat. Hettie did a quick count, finding one available double seat, which was lucky, because without Patty there was no tour. To avoid any further 'situations', as Poppa put it, it was decided that Tilly would take on the role of Patty's minder in addition to her responsibilities for costumes and stage management. Tilly was thrilled with her promotion, while Patty was just pleased to have a pair of eyes to guide her away from life's insurmountable hurdles – or at least to help her jump over them.

Chapter Five

Having settled the seating and accommodation issues, the tour party clambered off the bus and back into the Methodist Hall to rejoin Patty, who had finally made it down from the stage. Boobah – exhilarated from the bus ride – called her dancers to order and, as Enya thumped out a set of Irish jigs on her keyboard, the troupe came to life, executing the most complex of steps to perfection. They were clearly ready for a paying audience, so Poppa suggested they pack up for the day, since Patty and her band had more numbers to rehearse – and Enya's keyboard style was beginning to get on everyone's nerves. Bruiser offered to run the dancers back to their temporary digs in the town, keen to put the bus through its paces and make sure that there were no other mechanical problems.

Back on stage, Patty's band was 'getting it together', although there was a simmering dispute over how loud Deirdre's guitar should be. Patty claimed that she was 'cranking up her stack' while no one was looking, and Tilly was fascinated by the language. She decided to take Patty's side on all things and made a mental note to keep her eye on Deirdre, making sure that her paw didn't wander towards the volume control. Suzi Quake chimed in with a rather peevish comment about Alice's drums drowning everything out anyway, and suggested a Perspex screen to reduce the on-stage volume. Alice's reaction to the insult was swift: unleashing a string of expletives, she slammed her sticks down on her snare drum, leapt off the stage and proceeded to treat herself to a catnip roll-up. She then rejoined the band, in a much calmer state of mind, to run through a couple of Patty's quieter achievements.

Poppa was in his element as sound engineer and allowed the band's disputes to wash over him, having heard it all before. Musicians had come and gone from Hettie's band with alarming regularity, as she steered her autocratic way through the vagaries of the music business, and a tour without tantrums was no tour at all. He had to smile to himself as he remembered the moment when Hettie had sacked her entire band for overdoing the catnip at a summer festival, way back in the mists of time. She had been right, of course; the music was everything, and any band member who overstepped the line had to be dispatched without ceremony. Poppa smiled again at the realisation that Hettie hadn't changed: she might be a little older now, but she applied the same rules to her detective business, always pushing and moving forward until the job was done. He was pleased that their friendship had endured, and even more pleased to have her by his side on this tour.

Hettie was enjoying herself, too. Watching the interaction of Patty's band brought a flood of memories back: breaking in a new album, worrying about whether or not the fans would like the new songs, being nice to the fat cats from the record company when they bothered to turn up for a gig. Auditioning session players bored her to tears, but she had never truly found a cat she wanted to work with permanently, and anyway, her music was constantly changing direction and always needed fresh blood. It had been painful to give it up, but she'd gone out at the top of her game and was pleased not to have lingered long enough to tread into 'has-been' territory. Several years had passed, but Hettie was comforted by the realisation that nothing much had changed: the same rows, the same egos and the same anxieties were alive and kicking in Patty Sniff's band. Like Poppa, she had been there before, lived the life and collected all the T-shirts.

'I've just had a thought,' said Tilly, joining Poppa and Hettie at the mixing desk while Alice Slap completed another rock ending, kicking her cymbals over and missing Patty by inches. 'What about catering? There are too many of us to afford cafés on the road, and we haven't got proper facilities on Derek's bus.'

Poppa looked at Hettie, and she looked back at him. Tilly looked at them both and waited. When the answer came, it was a joyous one. In unison, Hettie and Poppa bellowed out a name which made Tilly clap her paws in sheer delight: 'Marley Toke!'

Marley Toke had arrived on the Catrush from Jamaica and had set herself up as a travelling cook around the music festivals, serving up the best street food that any cat could desire. Her jerk chicken was legendary, and most of her dishes were laced with her own homegrown catnip. Hettie and Poppa had passed many a happy hour in Marley's canteen of delights, before a food health scare forced her to disappear for a while. When the heat died down, she took a position as cook in the town's home for elderly cats until a spate of body snatching and murder caused the home to be sold. Tilly got to know Marley when she and Hettie were called in to investigate; it had been their very first case and, more by luck than judgement, they had triumphed. Afterwards, Marley had moved on to pastures new, setting up a guest house by the sea, and regularly invited Hettie and Tilly to spend a holiday with her in the sunshine. 'Do you think she'll come to our rescue?' asked Tilly. 'She's probably got a house full of guests and can't get away, especially at this time of year.'

'Well, there's only one way to find out,' said Hettie. 'When Bruiser gets back from dropping the dancers off, we'll have a spin out to Southwool in Miss Scarlet. I might even treat you to an ice cream.'

There was a crash from the back of the hall, as Derek and Belisha staggered through the door with a very large parcel. Belisha collapsed under the weight of it, and Poppa left his mixing desk to help Derek drag her out from the offending item. Hettie watched with wry amusement as the rotund cat was pulled free. Her red mac got caught in the crush and her miniskirt was up around her ears, leaving very little to the imagination. Derek clucked round her, concerned that there may be permanent damage – not to Belisha, but to the parcel he was looking forward to unpacking.

'What on earth have you got there?' asked Hettie, giving the parcel a prod with her paw. 'Not another box of magic tricks, is it?'

Adjusting her clothing for decency's sake, Belisha replied – as usual – on Derek's behalf. 'This 'ere is a magic box for our grand finale. 'Oudini 'ad one of these, so it's top of the range.'

Derek stripped the packing away to reveal a collapsible oblong box, and pulled it up to its full height so that it stood slightly taller than he was. It was painted a deep blue and decorated with silver stars, and it certainly looked more professional than the rest of Derek's tricks. The door was punctuated from top to bottom with tiny slits.

'So what does it do?' said Hettie, wanting to be impressed but not feeling very hopeful.

Belisha was thrown off guard by Hettie's question, as she had no idea what the magic box was capable of. She started searching through the discarded packing for the instructions, but Derek came to her rescue. 'It makes cats disappear,' he declared boldly, 'and lots of other stuff as well.'

'Excellent!' said Poppa, trying to sound enthusiastic, as Belisha emerged from the packing without the slightest hint of an instruction. She had managed to uncover a set of six trick daggers and a nasty-looking saw, though, and she threw them to one side to investigate later. 'Are we going to get a demo?'

Derek was wearing his uncertain face but blundered on, hoping for a miracle 'Well, if one of you would like to step inside the box, I'll show you what it can do.'

Tilly stepped forward, only to be pushed out of the way by Belisha. 'I'm the assistant. I'm the one who's goin' to disappear.'

Hettie resisted the obvious retort and watched as Belisha wedged herself inside the box. Derek shut the door on her. By that point, he had a captive audience, as The

Cheese Triangles and Patty had left the stage to see what was happening – or, in Patty's case, to 'feel the vibe'. Derek took up his magic wand and tapped the sides, then the back, and finally the front of the box. Not knowing exactly what to do next, he muttered, 'Abracadabra,' and invited Tilly to open the door. As everyone expected, Belisha Beacon was still wedged inside the box, very visible to her audience.

'I think that may need a bit more work, Derek,' said Poppa, returning to his mixing desk. Tilly helped Patty back up onto the stage, explaining to her what hadn't just happened, and Suzi and Deirdre tuned up for another session with Alice. Hettie headed for the door to see if there was any sign of Bruiser and the bus.

It would be late into the night before Derek and Belisha discovered the secret mechanism that made the magic box work, and by then no one cared one way or another. They decided to leave the saw and daggers for another day.

Chapter Six

It was a beautiful summer's evening, and still very warm. Bruiser gave Miss Scarlet full throttle as he headed out of the town towards the coast, and Hettie and Tilly enjoyed the exhilaration of the wind blowing through their long tabby fur as they sat back in the sidecar, singing at the top of their voices: 'Oh, we do like to be beside the seaside…'

Marley Toke's guest house was on the seafront, close to the pier-end of the beach. Bruiser parked the motorbike in a space directly in front of the three-storey clapboard villa. 'It's lovely,' said Tilly, 'but it must be lots of work. Look at all those windows! It's more like a hotel. Are you sure this is the right place?'

Hettie checked the address which Marley had scribbled on the back of a Christmas card. 'Yes, this is it, all right. She's done well for herself, hasn't she? But I doubt she'll be able to help us with the tour. Look at that sign in the window by the door – it says "No Vacancies".'

Tilly slumped down in her seat, disappointed, as Bruiser looked at Hettie and waited for instructions. 'Well, now we're here, the least we can do is say hello,' she said, struggling out of the sidecar. Tilly followed and the three friends beat a path to Marley's sunshine-yellow front door. Hettie could hear the strains of music coming from inside and was pleased that their journey hadn't been entirely wasted. She knocked and waited, then knocked and waited again, while Tilly decided to take a look through one of the front bay windows. She was immediately rewarded by a large black Rasta cat waving at her. Within seconds, he appeared at the door.

'Hey, me sorry not to hear,' he said, blinking at his three visitors, 'but we havin' me steel band practice an' dem drums put out big, big sound.'

Hettie smiled at the Jamaican cat, wondering whether Marley had finally found a soulmate. 'We came to visit Marley,' she explained. 'We're old friends, and we were just passing and thought we'd look her up. I'm Hettie, and these are Tilly and Bruiser.'

'An' you can call me Ludo,' said the black cat, offering a smile that Tilly thought was going to gobble her up. 'I tink you passed Marley. She down on de beach at her food shack. She do good business down dere at dis time of day. All dem hungry cats, dey can't get enough of her good cookin'. Just head for de pier, an' you'll see her big painted truck. It say "Marley's" on de side. You can't miss it.'

Hettie thanked Ludo, who returned to his steel drums, and the three cats crossed the road and walked down onto the sand. Ludo had been right: there was no missing the large army truck, now painted up with exotic Caribbean fruits and vegetables, catnip leaves, and – most importantly – the word 'Marley's' in bold curvy letters. Hettie led the way and Tilly tried hard to keep up. The sand and pebbles made progress difficult for her arthritic joints, but the smell of jerk chicken drove her on and Bruiser offered his paw when things became a little too painful.

Until then, Hettie had always thought that Elsie Haddock's fish-shop queue was the longest in the world, but Marley Toke's customers had brought deckchairs and beach mats. They waited patiently in the evening sun, smoking their catnip, chatting with the cats in front of them and generally hanging out at what was probably the coolest food vendor in town. 'What shall we do?' asked Tilly, slightly out of breath. 'She won't have time to talk to us with all these cats waiting for food.'

'Well, I don't know about anyone else, but I'm starving,' said Hettie. 'I think we should just join the queue. While we're waiting, we could have that ice cream I promised you, as a starter.' Bruiser offered to go for the ice creams, waving Hettie's money away and insisting that it was his treat. He set off for the promenade, where there were several ice cream vans to choose from.

The queue moved quicker than Hettie expected, and they had only just finished their ice creams when Marley's substantial figure loomed into view. The old army vehicle had been customised, and one side revealed an open-and-shut serving hatch where the cook reigned supreme. Her trademark giant hoop earrings swung as she slammed paper plate after paper plate of delicious food down on the ledge, and her delighted customers pounced on their orders.

They were close enough now to see the blackboard menu. Hettie was concerned that a number of the dishes had already been crossed through, but she was pleased to see that the fried chicken wings were still available, served with

Marley's special Jamaican dip. Any dish preceded by the word 'Jamaican' meant that it was heavily laced with home-grown catnip, and that's what Hettie was going for. Bruiser decided to do the same, but Tilly – who had never got on with catnip in any form – decided to go for beef strips in sweet potato pancakes with a squirt of tomato sauce.

Marley took Hettie's order without looking up, and it was only when she returned to the counter from her fryer that she recognised her old friend. 'Why, all my days, Miss Hettie!' she exclaimed. 'What a lovely surprise! And Miss Tilly, too – and who is dis handsome boy you hangin' out wid?'

Bruiser gave Marley an almost toothless grin, as she passed him his sizzling chicken wings. 'This is Bruiser,' Hettie said. 'He's an old friend, and now he drives us about in our motorbike and sidecar, and helps with our detective work.'

Marley beamed at Bruiser. 'Well, you sound like you got de best job, drivin' dees girls around – an' detectin' too! Dream job, me tinks.'

Bruiser was about to respond but the cats behind were getting a little fed up with the grand reunion, and Hettie – feeling the pressure at her back – passed Tilly her food and collected her own chicken wings, counting out the right money. Marley pushed the coins away. 'Me not takin' dat. You done plenty nice tings for me, so enjoy some Marley cookin' and then maybe we can sit a while an' catch up when I shut me shack up. Me runnin' outa everyting, so I won't be long.'

Hettie and Bruiser settled in the sand to eat their food. Tilly was a little late joining them, thanks to an incident with Marley's tomato sauce bottle. At first it had refused to dispense anything – no matter how hard she squeezed – and then suddenly the bottle seemed to take on a life of its own, squirting not just Tilly's dinner, but also a family of four kittens and an ageing granny who had been peacefully knitting in her deckchair, waiting to enjoy the sunset. The kittens collapsed into fits of giggles, as they raced to the sea to wash the sauce off, while the granny cat – pleased that the ketchup had missed her knitting – licked the sauce off her paws and face, and offered Tilly an appreciative glimpse of her gums. Tilly finally sat down in the sand and set about her pancakes. Bruiser and Hettie were sucking on their chicken bones, making sure that every drop of Jamaican dip was scraped from their plates. As predicted, by the time they had eaten their meals, Marley had finished serving and there was much banging of pans from inside her truck, as she packed up for the evening.

The sun was nowhere near ready to set and still offered some warmth as it shone over the sea, but the fierce heat of the day had been replaced by a balmy summer's evening. Hettie stretched out on the sand with her paws behind her head, watching the sea twinkle in the distance. Many of the cats with kittens were packing up their buckets and spades, beach umbrellas, wet bathing suits and windbreaks, ready to trudge back to their lodgings, and a whole new society of cats descended onto the beach with rugs, guitars, bags of food, lanterns and candles. Hettie watched as some of the groups gathered dry seaweed and branches ready to light small fires when the sun finally folded up her rays for the day.

'Look at those lovely beach huts over there,' said Tilly. 'That blue-and-red striped one is all fitted out with bunks, and they're having a barbecue on the veranda. I think we should have a beach hut next summer. Fancy waking up to the sound of the sea every day?'

Hettie thought about it for a moment before offering the flipside of the coin. 'What happens when the weather kicks off? I wouldn't want to be on this beach in a storm, and then there's the sand, of course – it gets in everywhere. And what if you don't like the cats on either side of your hut? Just think: you're stuck with them. They might have late-night parties to keep you awake, or worse – you might be murdered in your bunk. Anyway, it would be much nicer to stay at Marley's. You could still hear the sea, and you'd be guaranteed a decent breakfast.'

Tilly felt a little crushed by Hettie's thoughts on beach huts. She was older than she wanted to be, but her spirit of adventure was still very much alive and Hettie had had lots of adventures in her time; she'd even lived in a shed up on the town's allotments until the great storm had blown it away. Tilly knew that Hettie's bluster meant nothing, but she couldn't help thinking that she was becoming a little staid in her middle years – not that she would dream of telling her so.

'Now den!' said Marley, thundering across the sand in her huge open-toed sandals. 'Get your chops round dees: me best chocolate brownies and a bowl of Jamaican cream to dip dem in.'

Hettie sat up as Marley collapsed on the sand next to her, putting the tray of brownies in the middle so that everyone could reach them. Tilly went first, avoiding the bowl of cream which was dotted with green flecks of catnip; Hettie embraced both dishes, and Bruiser – knowing that he would have to drive home – allowed himself just a thin layer of cream.

Hettie had always enjoyed a pipe or two of catnip. It was a pleasure she'd adopted during her music days, when everyone who was anyone smoked or ate it. The plant was conducive to seeing the world in another form and turning life's mysteries upside down, and she had written some of her best songs while under its influence – even though in sober moments she had no idea what they were about. These days, it was just nice to slow things down and appreciate what would normally race by. It was a culture that Marley had been born with on her Jamaican island and many had tried to brand it a plant of the devil for its mind-altering properties, but for Hettie and many other cats it was just the calming balm to a busy, often hectic, life. She felt very serene as she stared out across the sea, watching the giant red ball of the sun begin to sink low onto the horizon. The sky was streaked with livid trails of red, pink and muted purple, as the day made way for the night, and little fires began to spring up across the beach, creating a truly magical scene. Hettie was so mesmerised by the picture before her that she'd quite forgotten the mission they were on, and it was Tilly who bravely raised the subject.

'Poppa is organising a tour for Patty Sniff—' she began, only to be interrupted by Marley.

'Oh dat Poppa boy! How is he doin'? I taut he was bein' a plumber or sometink? What he doin' messin' with Patty Sniff? She still goin'?'

'Yes,' said Tilly. 'She's just made a new record, and Poppa's organised a tour for her with some Irish dancers and a magician called Psycho Derek.'

'Psycho Derek!' exclaimed Marley. 'Not *de* Psycho Derek? He still kickin' around, tryin' to be famous and a magician, you say?'

'Not exactly,' said Hettie, joining in. 'In fact, not at all, judging by what we've seen at rehearsals today. But he's supplying the tour bus, so we're stuck with him and his bloody assistant, Belisha Beacon.'

Marley threw her large paws up in the air, causing her many bangles to slide up her arms as she bellowed with laughter. 'You sure got yourselves in de jar of pickled mangos over dis one. I take it you all goin' on dis tour wid Poppa boy?'

Hettie nodded. 'We do seem to be up to our necks in it, which is why we came to see you. We were going to ask if you'd do the catering, but you're obviously too busy with your guest house and your food shack.'

'Bless you for tinkin' of me. When do we leave?'

Hettie's jaw dropped, and Tilly and Bruiser stopped chewing on their brownies. 'You mean you'll come with us, even though it starts on Monday?'

'Any day's good for me. Me had enough of me beach shack dis summer. No time to tink, slavin' away in me truck. A change of scenery would be good for me, just like de old times.'

'But what about your guest house?' asked Tilly.

'Dat's not a problem. Me stopped havin' guests at de end of last summer. Me got fed up wid dem tramplin' all over de house – fur in me plugholes, kitten food up me walls, comin' an' goin' at all times, complainin' about de weather as if I'd planned it wet. I said to meself: Marley, dat's no way to live. I growin' slightly grey and me deserves some days in de sunshine, so I bought me an old army truck and done it up over de winter. Now I have me beach shack in the evenings and me sits in de sun all day.'

'But what about Ludo? Isn't he a guest?' said Hettie.

Marley laughed. 'Bless you, no! Dat Ludo boy is me nephew. Me sister Miriam sent him to me for Christmas, all de way from Jamaica. She said he needed educatin', but he's a good boy an' he fills dat big old house wid music. Since me best friend Alma fell off the pier and drowned, I been a bit lonely, but Ludo lets de sunshine in again. He started up a mighty fine steel band in de spring, and now he booked most weekends.'

Hettie was interested to know more about Alma, who had been involved in one of their earlier cases, but decided not to intrude on Marley's grief. Instead, she decided to talk practicalities regarding the tour. 'We leave on Monday. Will you be happy to take your truck? I don't think we have space on the bus.'

'Me fine widdat. Me follow in convoy. How long will we be away?'

'I think about ten days, if all the gigs come off and Patty lasts that long. Then there's The Cheese Triangles – not the calmest of temperaments, so it could all go paws up before we even get to West Grunting Pavilion on Monday night.'

'My dear Miss Hettie, always de optimist! If we got two days to get ready, me better call it a night. I need to get cookin' an plannin' me meals. How many me cookin' for?'

Hettie did a quick count on her paws and ran out of claws. 'About seventeen at the last count, but who knows what will have happened by Monday.'

It was dark as the friends left the beach. Marley fired up her truck and drove it back to her house, where she parked it in the driveway. Hettie and Tilly said their farewells, promising to phone over the weekend with the final arrangements, and clambered into the sidecar. Bruiser turned Miss Scarlet around and the three cats headed back to the town, pleased that their mission had been accomplished.

Chapter Seven

Saturday morning began early for Tilly: as soon as the Butters' bread ovens fired up, she sprang out of her blankets. The small room at the back of the bakery doubled as their detective agency by day and a comfortable bedsitter by night. The room boasted its own open fireplace, much used over the winter months; a tall, three-drawer filing cabinet; a large and cumbersome sideboard; a desk; a small sink and work surface, accommodating a kettle and pop-up toaster; and Hettie's armchair, where she was currently pretending to be fast asleep.

Tilly busied herself tidying away her blankets into the sideboard, where she stored everything that wasn't immediately needed. She filled and switched the kettle on, prepared her favourite mug with milk and a tea bag, and put two slices of bread in the toaster. She stood by the kettle, staring out at the garden and waiting for it to boil. Although it was supposed to switch itself off, she didn't trust it and it was the same with the toaster: some days it didn't toast the bread at all, whereas others it seemed to burn the bread on purpose. Tilly found it hard to accept the fast pace of the modern world. She loved her television but it had taken her some time to come to terms with their video machine, and the fact that it recorded her favourite programmes while she and Hettie were out on a case was more like magic to her than science. More recently, they'd acquired an answering machine for their phone, which caused great excitement until Hettie discovered that the only cat to use it was Tilly, who couldn't resist phoning it up whenever she went out, just for the sheer joy of hearing her own messages when she came home.

Tilly made the tea, spread her almost-brown toast with a thick layer of butter and padded across to the desk. Pulling a sheet of paper from the drawer, she settled to writing one of her lists, stopping occasionally to lick the butter off her toast and take a sip of tea. Tilly was more organised than Hettie gave her credit for, and had proved a huge asset to their detective agency. She loved making lists, poring over documents and taking notes, and had a knack for making connections where there appeared to be none. She put her talent down to the work of Miss Agatha Crispy, one of her favourite novelists, whose books she devoured, solving the crimes before Miss Crispy had had a chance to drag the body out of the library. Today the list was a pleasure to write, as it didn't include suspects, but nice things they needed for the tour.

Hettie rarely opened an eye before nine and never rose from her armchair until ten – if at all in the winter – but the smell of hot buttered toast was irresistible. She lifted her head, stretched, yawned and threw off her covers.

'Oh good,' said Tilly, skipping over to the kettle. 'Tea and toast? We've run out of cheese triangles, so it'll have to be butter.'

'Don't talk to me about cheese triangles! I dreamt about them all last night. They were at this gig and Patty had gone missing, so Boobah had to do the vocals. The best bit was when Belisha Beacon got electrocuted and turned bright orange before Psycho Derek sawed her body in half.'

'I'm not sure Marley's Jamaican dip agrees with you,' said Tilly, balancing two heavily buttered slices of toast on the arm of Hettie's chair and passing her a mug of milky tea.

'Well, fancy calling yourselves The Cheese Triangles anyway. It's not exactly new wave, is it?'

'Popular with cats, though,' countered Tilly. 'I don't think I've ever met a cat who doesn't like a cheese triangle.'

Hettie wanted to move on from the source of her nightmare and spent some time licking the butter off her toast, before eating the bread and settling to some serious whisker, paw and ear cleaning. Tilly continued with her list, ready to discuss its contents with Hettie when she finally rose from her bed. She was making slow progress: the hot summer weather made it difficult to know what and what not to take, and the lack of space on Derek's bus would prove a challenge. As always, food would have to be a major consideration; even with Marley supplying the main meals, they would still need in-between snacks and late-night suppers, which meant that she would have to make a separate list to give to Betty and Beryl. Meat pies and pasties would be out because of the heat, but their bakery offered an astonishing array of tasty treats which would travel and last at least a few days. She put crisps at the top of the Butters' list and worked through all their favourite treats from there, filling a whole page. Turning the paper over, she made a list of basic things they wouldn't want to be without. Leaving the lists for Hettie's approval and additions, she clambered down from the desk to assault the bottom drawer of the filing cabinet where they kept their clothes.

'I suppose it's just T-shirts for this trip,' she said, disappearing under a mountain of summer outfits. 'Are we going grunge or tabby chic?'

Hettie joined Tilly at the filing cabinet and the two friends worked their way through several choices. Hettie opted for some of her favourite T-shirts, all offering social and not-so-social comments across the front. Tilly went for book titles and then changed her mind when she found the three *Top Cat* T-shirts that Hettie had bought for her birthday. She loved *Top Cat* and his rabble of street cats, and decided that it might give her an urban edge to be seen in one. Not that she entirely knew what an urban edge was, but she'd heard Patty Sniff say it and thought it sounded nice.

When the clothes had been selected and placed in a pile on the desk, Hettie turned her attention to Tilly's lists and realised that she couldn't read a word of them. Tilly's paws were large and flat, which made holding a pencil difficult, and the fact that she really needed glasses was another contributing factor to the hotchpotch of letters which danced before Hettie's eyes. 'I think you'd better read this out,' she said. 'It looks like the work of a maniac.'

Tilly snatched the paper from Hettie's paw, choosing to read the food list first. 'I've decided to get all the food from the Butters to save time on shopping, so it's mostly treats. Crisps, obviously. Ring doughnuts, cheese straws, flapjacks, cheese scones, chocolate muffins, jam tarts, some of those iced biscuits we like, a Swiss roll with pretend cream and some egg custards. I've had to steer clear of fresh cream and meat – unless Derek's got a fridge on his bus?'

'I think we're lucky it's got wheels, let alone a fridge. Let's order some pies for the first day – they'll be fine if we eat them on the way to West Grunting Pavilion. Better order four steak-and-kidneys, as Bruiser and Poppa will need something.'

Tilly added the pies to her list and was about to rattle through the general requirements for the tour when a muffled ringing came from the staff sideboard, where the phone was kept. She abandoned her list and scrambled inside. Hettie hated phones almost as much as she hated most other cats, and the concept of a stranger breaking into her personal space when she was least expecting it was just too much for her. She knew her detective business needed a telephone, but keeping it muffled in cushions and out of sight was the only way she could cope. Tilly always answered it, anyway, as Hettie – even if she shed several pounds – would never fit into the sideboard.

'Hello, the No. 2 Feline Detective Agency, Tilly speaking. Oh, hello Poppa. Would you like to speak to Hettie?' Tilly backed out of the sideboard, bringing the telephone with her, and handed the receiver to her friend. Hettie had hardly said hello before Poppa launched into a tale of woe, with Hettie responding whenever she could.

'She's what? She can't be! A bacon sandwich? I don't believe it! So what are we going to do now? OK, we'll see you there at eleven.'

Hettie gave the receiver back to Tilly, who had been waiting patiently for news. 'It's Alice Slap,' she explained. 'She choked on a bacon sandwich last night. Deirdre and Suzi found her this morning, dead in her bed. Poppa's calling a meeting at the Methodist Hall at eleven to see what's to be done, but it looks like the tour's off.'

* * *

Poppa was the first to arrive at the Hall, swiftly followed by Hettie, Tilly and Bruiser. 'Bit of a sod, all this,' Poppa said, trying to come to terms with the news.

'How did you find out?' Hettie asked.

'Deirdre Nightshade turned up at me narrowboat first thing this morning. I thought it was a joke to start with, but then she started sobbing and carrying on. They're staying at Hilary and Cherry Fudge's house; they take in guests in the summer to make a few extra bob – they even let Derek park his bus in their driveway.'

Hettie knew Hilary and Cherry well. The mother and daughter cats gave their enthusiasm to many of the town's events and had, in their time, administered first aid to both Bruiser and Tilly during one of the No. 2 FDA's more serious cases. It occurred to Hettie that offering accommodation to a female punk band was a little outside their normal comfort zone, not to mention having Derek's art gallery on wheels parked in their driveway, but she decided to let Poppa continue with the details of Alice Slap's unfortunate departure from the land of the living.

'Deirdre said that they'd all gone out late to get some supper from Greasy Tom's fast food van. Most of them had burgers, but Patty and Alice ordered bacon sandwiches.'

'When you say most of them, who was there?' interrupted Hettie.

'Well, as far as I understand it, everyone went to Greasy Tom's except Patty. She stayed behind and waited in her room, which she was sharing with Alice. The Irish lot are staying next door with Finbar O'Leary and his old mother. They all went to Tom's, too.'

'But how did Alice manage to choke to death? Didn't anyone try to help her?' Tilly asked.

'According to Deirdre, Patty thought she heard Alice coughing in the night but didn't realise there was a problem. Obviously, anyone who could see would have known that Alice was struggling; instead, Patty ate her own bacon sandwich and went to sleep. Deirdre said that Alice had an issue with food and always ate too quickly. She said it was a throwback to being raised with eight other kittens, all fighting for food.'

'Where's Alice now?' asked Hettie.

'Hilary called Shroud and Trestle to come and pick her up. They're getting in touch with one of her sisters.'

'So what's the plan? Patty can't go on without a drummer, so that's your main act gone, and I don't think they'll be queuing round the block to see Derek and a troupe of Irish dancers.'

With a heavy heart, Poppa agreed, acknowledging that the tour was definitely off.

'It's such a shame,' piped up Tilly, 'especially as Marley said she could come with us. I was looking forward to living on a bus for a few days.'

'That sounds like the bus now,' said Bruiser. 'I'll go and 'elp 'em get the wheelchair off. Bit of a steep slope that ramp, and we don't want any more disasters.'

The touring party alighted with very little enthusiasm, shocked and saddened by the news of Alice's death. There was nothing particularly heroic about choking on a bacon sandwich, and when the story hit the music press, Alice's death would go down not in glory but as one of life's unfortunate mishaps. Tilly went with Bruiser to guide Patty into the hall and Boobah was last off the bus, freewheeling down her ramp with an unaccustomed squeal of excitement.

Poppa waited until everyone was assembled before announcing the bad news. 'I'm afraid the tour is cancelled. There's no way we can go on without Alice.'

''Ang on,' said Belisha. 'Are you tellin' me that Magical Mystery Paws won't be appearin' cos some greedy little cymbal-basher 'as choked 'er stupid self? What about my Derek? 'E's just got the 'ang of the magic box, an' now you're tellin' us it's all off?'

Derek looked embarrassed and the rest of the company was horrified by Belisha's outburst, but it was Cormac who stepped forward, raising his paw to attract Poppa's attention. 'I've done a bit of stick work in my old da's band back in Donegal. Surely I could try the drums in Patty's band? I've got all her records, and I tink I could manage if I had a bit of practice.'

'You are joking, aren't you?' said Suzi Quake, eying the dancer up and down. 'You're hardly big enough to see over Alice's drum kit, let alone hit it with any force. You need attitude to play this music. Bobbing up and down in ballet shoes doesn't do it for me.'

Cormac stared down at his dancing shoes, wishing he hadn't stepped forward at all, but it was Patty who spoke up for him. 'The least we can do is give him a go. We've got the rest of today and all day tomorrow to work him in, and if we don't shift some albums on this tour we're sunk.'

Deirdre agreed with Patty, more to spite Suzi than to support Cormac, but Boobah insisted on having her say in her best French and slightly Russian accent. 'And vot am I to do with only five dancers and Enya? Ve have already lost one, and now my principal dancer is leaving us to be in a pop group!'

'But I can do both,' protested Cormac. 'I promise I'll work really hard, so I will.'

Boobah thought for a moment and then gave in. 'Very vell, but I vill beat you blue and black if you let me down.'

Poppa had stayed out of the arguments, but as now it seemed that there was a slim possibility that the tour was back on, he decided to get everyone back to rehearsals. Derek and Belisha were sent to a corner of the hall, where Derek was keen to have a go at sawing Belisha in half, but settled instead for pinning her inside the magic box with retractable daggers. Boobah took the centre of the hall for a warm-up set of jigs, while Cormac climbed onto the stage and settled himself behind Alice's drum kit, offering the widest of Irish smiles as a cat who had definitely got the cream. Whether the cream was about to curdle remained to be seen.

Chapter Eight

Deirdre and Suzi struggled with their new bandmate to start with. Neither of them had particularly liked Alice Slap, but there was a sisterhood of sorts in The Cheese Triangles. Their gigs as Patty Sniff's backing band had rocketed them into the mainstream, and doing the sessions on her new album had cemented them in a world where anything was possible. Suzi had already started writing her own songs, mostly inspired by Patty's back catalogue, and Deirdre had shown some talent for making up tunes. The plan was to get Patty's tour out of the way, advertise for a vocalist, work in the new songs on the pub circuit and make their own album. Annoyingly, Alice had remained fiercely loyal to Patty for giving The Cheese Triangles their big break. Suzi and Deirdre sometimes forgot that Patty was a star and had a track record to prove it. She had risen from the ashes, mostly of her own making, on several occasions and quite often against all odds; singing was the only joy she possessed, the only thing that she didn't have to see to believe in, and Suzi and Deirdre had a very long way to go before – in Patty's words – they 'got the trip'.

Cormac's first few faltering beats were soon replaced by a consistent hammering out of the rhythms set up by Suzi and Deirdre, as Patty Sniff's vocal attack drove the music on. By the time the band broke for lunch, Cormac looked every bit the punk drummer, twirling his sticks and even standing up at one point to deliver a pounding tom-tom solo in the middle of Patty's big hit, 'Slack Off'. Hettie was impressed but felt that the uniform green tabard, which Boobah insisted the dance troupe wore, did little for Cormac's street cred; she suggested he pop into Jessie's charity shop to choose something black, perhaps with studs. Tilly was keen to get back to her lists, and Hettie felt that a Butters' pie would go a long way to bridging the gap between breakfast and dinner. The two friends made their way home, leaving Bruiser to tinker with Derek's bus. Poppa was still pacing the floor in the Methodist Hall, waiting for the arrival of the tour merchandise and the first copies of Patty's new album, *Sausage and Slash*.

By the time Hettie and Tilly reached the Butters' bakery, their lunchtime queue was dwindling but – as Hettie lamented – so were the pies. Betty and Beryl had built up their business entirely from word of mouth. Being in the town's High Street helped, but it was the sheer quality of their baking that made cats travel out of their way to carry home a pie or pastry in a Butters paper bag. When Betty and Beryl offered Hettie their back room, they included daily luncheon vouchers in the rent and as much coal from their stack in the yard as her fire would consume. Hettie wouldn't admit it but they had probably saved her life, offering food, shelter and warmth;

with their blessing, she had offered the same to Tilly. The arrangement worked well, and with Bruiser now installed in a shed at the bottom of the garden, the community was complete.

'I was wondering where you two had got to,' said Betty, decanting what was left of the cream cakes onto one tray. 'We've put a couple of minced beef and onion pies to one side for your dinner.'

'And Tilly's got her favourite,' chimed in Beryl. 'A cream horn, and a nice wedge of Victoria sandwich for Hettie.'

Betty fetched the two bags from the back of the shop and banged them down on the counter. 'Your vouchers will cover that. Anything else we can get you? We're closing early again because it's just too hot.'

Tilly suddenly remembered her food list and began to panic, realising that tomorrow was Sunday and that left very little time for the Butters to fulfil her order. 'We're doing a tour with Poppa,' she began, 'so we'll be away next week and we have a small list of things we'd like to take with us from the bakery, if that's not too much trouble? I'll go and fetch it, if you like.'

'Come on then,' said Beryl, lifting the counter so that Tilly could take the shortcut to the back of the shop. She returned seconds later, a little out of breath, and handed the list to Betty.

'Well, sister – just take a look at this! That's the biggest small list I've ever seen.'

Beryl took the list from Betty's paw and shook her head, offering a whistling noise through her teeth for dramatic effect before delivering the blow Tilly dreaded. 'Not a chance of getting this lot baked off by Monday, not with it being Sunday tomorrow. Trouble is, our ovens don't seem to work on Sundays, do they, sister?'

Tilly felt the first hot tears of frustration travelling down her nose before Beryl let out a huge boom of laughter. 'Dear me, did you really think we'd let you down? We'll have this lot all packed up and ready to go first thing Monday morning. We can't let you starve, can we, sister?'

Lifting the counter once again, Hettie and Tilly skipped through to their room, pleased to have the best landladies in town and forever grateful for their kindness in all things. 'These minced beef pies are huge,' said Hettie, tipping them out onto the desk. 'Shall we share one now and have the other for supper?'

There was no answer from Tilly. Hettie tore herself away from the pies and noticed that the staff sideboard door was open. 'What are you doing in there?' she asked.

'The light's flashing on the answering machine,' came Tilly's muffled reply. She eventually emerged with the telephone, the answering machine and a tangle of wires. 'There are three messages.'

'And how many of them have you left?' asked Hettie.

'None of them,' said Tilly, a little put out. 'I'll play them back to prove it isn't me.'

Tilly pressed the playback button and the machine sprang into life. 'Hi you two, Morbid Balm here. I need to speak to one of you urgently. Give us a callback when you get this.' The machine bleeped, introducing the second message. 'Hello, only me again. Got a bit of a situation which you might be interested in. Call me back.' The final message was a little more businesslike, as if someone had been listening at the other end. 'Hello, this is Morbid

Balm from Shroud and Trestle Undertakers. We have a client resting with us by the name of Alice Slap. She's down as an accidental death, but I'm afraid – on closer inspection – it would appear that she's been strangled with a guitar string.'

Chapter Nine

The business premises of Shroud and Trestle were tucked away at the bottom of Sheba Gardens. Like most undertakers, it was a family firm and had been serving the town for over a hundred years. It was taken for granted that there would always be a partnership between the two families as they passed the business on from father to son, but Morbid Balm was the exception. Her business card read: 'M. Balm, mortician and after-death makeover artist' – a modern concept for a tradition which had, in the past, treated its corpses with respect but done very little to enhance the look of its clients once they were in their coffins. Morbid changed all of that: having initially applied to be a pall-bearer, she had worked her way into the preparation room, where she performed her own brand of magic.

To look at her, there was no doubt that she favoured the Goth style. She was rarely seen in any colour but black, right down to her claws, which she painted every Thursday evening as a ritual of self-indulgence. Since Hettie set up the No. 2 Feline Detective Agency, their paths had crossed on a regular basis and Morbid had, on occasions, become part of Hettie's team. Having an experienced mortician on board during a murder case was invaluable, and Hettie and Tilly not only respected Morbid's opinion, but liked her attitude to her work. It seemed that Morbid's mission in life was to send cats to their graves looking the best they possibly could. With that in mind, she painstakingly replaced eyes, whiskers and the occasional ear, as well as shampooing and fluffing up the fur of the deceased as a matter of course. It was her attention to detail and her loyalty to Shroud and Trestle that made her part of the undertaking family – and she had, by her own merit, become the firm's biggest asset.

Bruiser parked Miss Scarlet in the undertaker's yard. Hettie and Tilly clambered out of the sidecar, leaving him to clamber in for a snooze in the morning sun. Tilly was generally spared the more macabre aspects of the detective business, but curiosity and a ride in Miss Scarlet had made her brave, and she was ready to face whatever Morbid chose to show them with a professional attitude. At least she hadn't had time to get to know Alice Slap, which would make viewing her body much easier.

'We've come to see Morbid Balm,' said Hettie to a pale, thin, short-haired cat at the reception desk.

The cat offered a clammy paw by way of formal greeting. 'And may I say that we at Shroud and Trestle are truly sad for your loss,' she said. 'We will do everything we can to offer you a smooth passage through your grief. I'll tell Miss Balm you're here, but in the meantime perhaps you'd like to take a seat and look through our ring file? The price list is at the back, and that includes the coffin furniture – handles, plaques and screw-downs to you and me.'

The cat had made some attempt at a light-hearted comment, but Hettie was still reeling from the touch of her paw, which had made her flesh creep. According to the badge she wore, the receptionist was a genuine Trestle, and Hettie wondered what that might be like. Spending your life around sad and dead cats, sharing the grief of others day after day until you eventually became one of them, seemed a dismal prospect.

'I wonder if she ever lets her hair down,' Hettie mused, as the cat deserted her post to go and look for Morbid. 'I can't imagine her enjoying a cream cake with her eyes shut in ecstasy. She looks like she's died and been dug up again.'

'I bet she doesn't watch *Top Cat,* either,' said Tilly, pawing through the wicker-coffin section of the ring file. 'I wouldn't want one of these. It's not worm-proof and the soil would get in.'

'I think that's the point,' said Hettie, as the receptionist returned.

'Miss Balm has a client with her at the moment, but she's asked me to take you through to the viewing room, if you'd care to follow me?'

Hettie and Tilly did as they were told and found themselves in a small, oak-panelled room, where a closed coffin rested on a central table. The room was heady with the scent of oriental lilies, and Tilly began to sneeze uncontrollably until Hettie pulled a tissue from a box by the flowers and forced it in front of her nose. The room had several chairs around the edge, and the two friends settled themselves down to wait for Morbid to conclude her business.

Tilly, finally over her sneezing fit, kept a wary eye on the coffin, expecting its lid to open at any moment. Hettie stared at a collection of framed photographs on the wall opposite, which chronicled the history of Shroud and Trestle. The pictures showed stern-looking Victorian cats posing against a shiny glass hearse, harnessed to a pair of very fine horses with dark plumes on their heads. The more up-to-date pictures with motor hearses seemed to have lost the grandness and romanticism of that different age, but strangely – as Hettie discovered on closer inspection – the same faces stared out of the photos, as if the Victorian undertakers had simply reinvented themselves in the family dynasty.

'Sorry about that,' said Morbid, bustling through the door and throwing a pile of clothes down onto one of the empty chairs. 'I got caught up in a wardrobe dispute. It's never easy to decide what to send 'em off in. I wish these conversations could be had when they're still alive. Old Horace Catchpole's been dying for twelve months on and off, so you'd think he might have had a moment to decide on what he wanted to be buried in instead of leaving it up to his daughter. She's in bits – can't get a sensible word out of her. Anyway, enough of my problems. I thought you'd be interested in taking a look at Alice Slap.'

Morbid crossed to the coffin and lifted the lid off, leaning it against the panelling. Hettie moved forward and Tilly hung back, preferring to view Alice at a more comfortable distance.

'On first sight,' said Morbid, 'it looked like a tragic accident. When I went to pick her up from the Fudges', she was lying in her bed with what was left of a bacon sandwich in her mouth. She had a blue look about her and her eyes were bulging. When I got her back here and set about tidying her up, I took the half-eaten sandwich out of her mouth and noticed that she hadn't even tried to swallow it. On further investigation, there was no bread or bacon in her throat, but the windpipe was constricted. Then I noticed this.' Morbid pulled a coiled piece of wire from her back pocket. 'It was so tightly pulled around her neck that it was obscured by her fur. I wouldn't have found it if I hadn't been brushing her. A neat job, really. Almost clever.'

Hettie took the piece of wire for closer inspection. 'Yes, it's a guitar string all right. Bronze wound, medium gauge, and a G or D string at a guess.'

Tilly and Morbid were impressed. For Hettie, the nightmare of changing her guitar strings back in the day had forged a lasting memory and led to an intimate knowledge of strings, machine heads and sound holes. Tilly moved closer to the coffin, trying to be brave. 'It's such a shame that she won't be coming with us on the tour,' she said. 'I thought she was really good.'

'What tour was that then?' asked Morbid, leaning into the coffin to tidy Alice's whiskers.

'She was one of The Cheese Triangles, Patty Sniff's backing band,' Tilly replied.

'Blimey! Not *the* Patty Sniff? I loved her stuff when I was going through me punk phase – just before I became a Goth, actually. I got fed up with all the spitting, though. I used to come home from her gigs covered in it. No wonder they all wore bin bags – at least you could wipe 'em down. So Alice was in Patty's band? Well, I never! I didn't realise we had a celebrity in the freezer – and speaking of that, I'd better put her back in. We don't want her decomposing, do we?'

Both Hettie and Tilly appreciated Morbid's rather off-colour joke, but time was ticking on and it would appear that they had a murder case on their paws. The big question was whether or not the tour should go ahead with a sadistic killer on the loose. Hettie and Tilly said their farewells to Morbid and joined Bruiser in the sunshine, pleased to shake off the sombre atmosphere of the undertaker's.

'Home for a think, calling in at the Methodist Hall and the Fudges' on the way,' said Hettie, as she and Tilly took up their seats in the sidecar. Bruiser kicked Miss Scarlet into life and the three cats sped off down Sheba Gardens in the direction of Cheapcuts Lane.

Conveniently, Poppa was sitting on the low wall outside the hall, taking a break from rehearsals, and Hettie wasted no time in imparting the news. 'We have a problem,' she began, looking round to make sure that none of the other tour personnel were in earshot. 'Alice Slap was murdered – not by a bacon sandwich, but by this.' She pulled the coiled guitar string from her back pocket and passed it to Poppa.

'Well, that's a real sod,' he said, turning the string in his paws. 'Bronze wound, medium gauge… a D string, I'd say. Acoustic, of course – too heavy for electric. Not the sort Deirdre would use on her Strat, although Derek and Tarmac have acoustic guitars with them. Not that that means anything.'

Tilly marvelled at Poppa's on-tour language, and vowed to ask him what a Strat was when things were a little less fraught. 'So what do we do now?' asked Hettie, putting the string back in her pocket. 'Should we cancel the tour or push on and hope that no one else hits the floor? The murderer is amongst us, I've no doubt about that, but they obviously think they're clever, fooling us into believing that Alice's death was an accident.'

Poppa thought for a moment, weighing up the pros and cons before responding. 'If we call it all off, we'll never catch who's done this. They'll all go home and that'll be that. If we go ahead, maybe the killer will reveal him- or herself.'

Hettie nodded in agreement. 'Yes, and if we carry on as if Alice's death was an accident, it'll be easier to keep an eye on everyone without raising suspicions.'

'But what if Alice was only the first on the list?' said Tilly.

'I think that's a risk we'll have to take. We'll have to regard everyone as a suspect, and at least we're one step ahead in knowing how Alice died. I'm keen to hear what the Fudges have to say about their house guests. Maybe they can shed some light on the comings and goings last night.'

Hettie, Tilly and Bruiser took off in the direction of Snuffle Walk, where Cherry and Hilary Fudge kept a very nice semi-detached house. Poppa turned on his heel and wandered back into the hall, looking like a cat with the troubles of the world on his shoulders.

Chapter Ten

Cherry Fudge was scrubbing her step as Bruiser parked Miss Scarlet in the driveway. So frenetic was her cleaning that she hardly noticed her visitors until Hettie stood in front of her. 'Oh, dear me!' she said, dipping her scrubbing brush into a soapy washing-up bowl. 'What a day it's been! Mother's always saying, "Cherry, you chew every bit before you swallow." That poor cat! I suppose she was hungry. These young cats never have time for a proper meal, dashing about and caught up in all sorts.'

Cherry Fudge carried on scrubbing the step that had never been dirty in the first place until Hettie gently removed the brush from her paw. She was clearly agitated and in shock. Hettie signalled to Bruiser to stay put while she and Tilly helped Cherry, the scrubbing brush and the washing-up bowl into the house and through to the kitchen, where Hilary had just rescued a tray of jam tarts from her oven. Hilary looked as disturbed as her daughter, and mumbled a greeting before slumping down on a kitchen chair.

'I'm sorry to call at such a difficult time,' said Hettie, 'but we wondered if you could tell us anything about last night and what happened to Alice Slap?'

'I blame Greasy Tom,' Hilary replied. 'It lowers the tone, bringing that old van round here – just encourages cats to go out late when there's food about.'

'What time did they go out?' asked Hettie. 'And who went?'

'Well, they all did, except the blind one. All that Irish lot went, too – they're staying next door, and they made such a racket. It was gone eleven, and they were all singing and dancing down the street. I said to Cherry, "We're not doing this again!" We like the quiet life. And then this morning those two were screaming their heads off as if someone had been murdered.'

Hettie shot a look at Tilly before continuing with her questions. 'Do you mean Deirdre Nightshade and Suzi Quake?'

'Yes, that's right – although I'd scream too if I had names like that. Then that big cat with the miniskirt who lives on the bus joined in, and before we knew it, the Irish lot were all round here as well, pushing their way into our best bedroom to take a look at that poor dead cat. The blind one behaved better. She just sat on her bed, rocking backwards and forwards. I blame it on the catnip, I really do.'

'Could we see the room where it happened?' asked Hettie.

'There's nothing to see now. Cherry even changed the sheets after the undertakers were gone, but you're welcome to go up, if you like. She will show you.'

Cherry Fudge led Hettie and Tilly upstairs, and stopped outside one of the doors on the landing. 'I won't come in, if that's all right. I need to get on with scrubbing the front step.'

Cherry's parting comment was more than a little disturbing, and Tilly wondered whether she should be included in the list of suspects that she would make in her notebook later. Hettie pushed the door open, keen to see where Alice Slap had been murdered. The room had twin beds, with matching eiderdowns and curtains; there was a bedside cabinet for each, with a cupboard and drawer for essentials. The bed on the right had been made in a hurry, and the pillow still bore evidence of having been recently slept on. Hettie assumed that this had been Patty Sniff's bed, because the other was made up within an inch of its life and not a crease in sight. She stared at Cherry's neat handiwork before looking inside the bedside cabinet, signalling for Tilly to take a look in the one allocated to Patty.

'Not much in here,' said Hettie, pulling out an open packet of liquorice allsorts and helping herself to a pink one with coconut. 'Sweets and a bag of make-up, but this might be interesting – there's a Filofax, shoved right to the back of the drawer.'

'Not a lot in here,' said Tilly. 'I wouldn't have taken Patty for being the religious type, though.'

'Why, what have you found?'

'A Bible – look!'

Hettie laughed and helped herself to another of Alice's sweets, this time choosing the one with the white centre. 'That'll be Gideon's Bible, not Patty's,' she said through a mouthful of liquorice.

'But who is Gideon? And why has he left his Bible in Patty's drawer?' asked Tilly, sorting through the bag of sweets for the blue one covered in hundreds and thousands, which was her favourite.

'As far as I know, Gideon was some religious warlord and a bunch of busybody cats in America decided that every hotel and guest house in the whole world should have a copy of his Bible in the drawer by the bed. I think they came from Nashville.'

'Why? Did Gideon come from Nashville? I wonder if he knew Pussy Parton?'

'Probably not,' said Hettie, realising that they were moving slightly off the beaten track.

'Well, I'd rather have an Agatha Crispy or a Nicolette Upstart in my drawer, if I was miles from home. Ooh, look, there's one of those Braille books in here. *The Scratcher in the Rye* – that must be Patty's, unless Gideon was blind as well as from Nashville.'

Hettie decided that it was time to move on before Tilly rewrote Gideon's and Nashville's history, using a logic that existed only in her world. 'Let's put all the stuff back where we found it, except for the Filofax and the liquorice allsorts.'

'Why are we keeping the sweets?' asked Tilly, running her paw over Patty's book with her eyes closed.

'So we can eat them. I don't think Alice would mind.'

Taking a quick look under each bed and finding not even a speck of dust, Hettie gathered up the Filofax and the sweets, and put the make-up bag back in the cupboard. Tilly put Patty's book back where she'd found it and the two tabbies took one last look round the place. As they were leaving, the room was suddenly filled with diesel fumes. The window was wide open and Hettie crossed to it. Looking down onto the Fudges' driveway, she was just in time to see the arrival of Derek's bus. 'Rehearsals are obviously finished for the day,' she said, 'but look how close the bus's roof is to this window. Anyone could have got in here last night if they'd climbed up on that roof. It was such a hot night, and I'd put money on this window being wide open. If the killer came in this way, it definitely points to one of the tour party who knew that Alice was sharing with Patty, and that Patty couldn't be a viable witness. We need to talk to her first, I think. She said she heard Alice choking, but she might have picked up something else like a noise or a smell. Blind cats are supposed to have some sort of heightened senses about them. You should tackle that one, as you're Patty's minder, but I think we'll wait until the tour gets under way. The killer will think they've got away with it, and hopefully will drop their guard.'

Tilly was pleased to be given the first investigative interview of the case, and was even more pleased that it was with Patty; after all, she was the star. The friends made their way back to the Fudges' kitchen, where Hilary was pounding a lump of dough in a large mixing bowl. Cherry had turned her attention from the front step to the kitchen windows, which were now obscured by a liberal application of Windolene. As they entered the room, Hilary took up from where she left off, as if they'd been there all along. 'And the shame of it is, Cherry didn't even get the chance to do her Heimlich manoeuvre. She's been practising it on herself for months – abdomen thrusts, they are. Put that cloth down, and show Hettie and Tilly how you do them, Cherry.'

Cherry responded immediately and took centre stage in the kitchen, balling one of her paws up into a fist. Forcing it under her ribcage and clasping the fist with her other paw, she pulled upward with a violent jerking movement. Hettie sidestepped the half-digested jam tart that shot out of Cherry's mouth, landing conveniently in the washing-up bowl by the sink.

'There you are,' continued Hilary. 'A textbook performance. She'd have shifted that bacon sandwich all right. You've got to do it quickly on account of the brain damage, you see, but no one called for help. She's doing severe burns and scalding next, aren't you, Cherry?'

Hettie decided that it was time to leave the town's first aiders to their remaining house guests. Deirdre Nightshade and Suzi Quake were loitering in the hallway while Patty felt her way up the stairs. When Hettie and Tilly shut the door behind them, they heard the strains of an argument coming from Derek's bus, where Belisha Beacon was treating those left on board to a shouting match. Boobah's wheelchair appeared to have broken free of her ramp, depositing the dance mistress amongst Hilary's dahlias. Bruiser and Enya did their best to retrieve her, while Belisha was keen for the rest of the dance troupe to vacate the bus as quickly as possible so that she could claw back some personal space – although she didn't put it quite that elegantly.

With Boobah safely returned to her wheelchair, Bruiser broke away from the chaos to drive Hettie and Tilly home. It had been a long and strange day, but Hettie suspected that there was much worse to come. Sitting in Miss Scarlet's sidecar with a cool breeze blowing through her fur, she couldn't help but feel that Alice Slap was the lucky one: any troubles she had were over, while theirs were probably just beginning. What she needed now was a pie, a cream cake and a pipe or two of catnip. After all, tomorrow was another day.

Chapter Eleven

Sunday was a busy day, full of last-minute arrangements and packing. Tilly rescued her tartan shopper from its parking space by the Butters' bread oven and gave it a cursory wipe round with a damp cloth, having decided that she was going to pack the food in it. She'd calculated that there would be a spare seat near her on the bus, where she could store the shopper for easy access. With the hot weather set to continue, they were taking very few clothes, although she made sure to pack her new poncho; the nights might be cold, and she didn't want to leave it at home on its own.

Hettie had shown very little interest in the packing, leaving most of it in Tilly's capable paws. Instead, she spent most of the day sitting on a deckchair in the sun, discussing the tour schedule and bus route with Bruiser and Poppa. At least, that's what she told Tilly she was doing, although on the two occasions when Tilly ventured down to the bottom of the garden, she found all three cats fast asleep in the sun.

Betty and Beryl had surprised them all by putting on a rather fine Sunday tea by way of wishing them bon voyage, and Tilly helped to carry it down the garden. It was quite some spread, and she insisted on identifying each lovely plateful as she put everything out on a picnic rug: 'Beef paste, salmon paste and chicken paste sandwiches, without the crusts; sausage rolls with cheese pastry; mini pork pies; egg and bacon tartlets; red and yellow cheese cubes on sticks; three bowls of crisps; and a flagon of Meridian Hambone's fiery ginger beer.'

Meridian Hambone was one of the oldest residents in the town. She kept a hardware shop in the High Street that sold everything *including* the kitchen sink, which had no doubt been rescued from the back of a lorry by her enterprising son, Lazarus. Exactly where the fiery ginger beer came from remained a mystery, but Meridian sold gallons of it every year to legions of very happy cats, who just kept coming back for more.

When Tilly had finished announcing the savouries, Betty wheeled the sweets out on a hostess trolley. There was some difficulty in getting the trolley to behave itself across the rough terrain of the Butters' lawn, and it was no surprise that several iced fancies broke free and bounced into the flower borders before the trolley reached its destination. Bruiser leapt up to retrieve them, blowing the soil off and popping them inside his shed for later.

Hettie looked admiringly at the savouries before encouraging Tilly to run through the contents of the sweet trolley. By now she had a captive audience, as Betty and Beryl had joined them, allowing Poppa and Bruiser to set up their fold-down chairs. Tilly cleared her throat and began, pointing to every item with her paw as she announced it: 'Iced fancies, in pink, lemon and white; custard slices; jam and cream split buns; chocolate eclairs; lemon curd tarts; chocolate fudge squares; cream horns; fruit scones and cherry scones, both with spread-it-yourself cream; and a very large trifle with chocolate dots and fresh cream.' Tilly took a bow as the cats applauded her presentation. There was very little conversation after that, although the audible lip-smacking and grunts of appreciation filled the silence.

The sun had gone down by the time Poppa said his farewells, arranging to pick Hettie, Tilly and Bruiser up in the morning at ten o'clock. The plan was for Derek to bring the bus with the performers and park it outside the post office opposite the bakery, while they waited for Marley Toke's truck to join them. Bruiser would then take over the driving of the bus, and the two vehicles would travel in convoy.

Tilly was overexcited and a little queasy, having had three cream horns during the tea party – a real milestone for her, as she'd only ever managed two in a single sitting before. The combination of the fiery ginger beer, three cream horns and her first road trip on tour with a band made sleep impossible, and her tossing and turning on the blanket began to get on Hettie's nerves. Hettie rubbed her eyes with her paw, sitting bolt upright in her chair. 'I completely forgot!' she exclaimed.

'What?'

'Alice Slap's Filofax!' Hettie stumbled to the desk, where she'd abandoned the liquorice allsorts and the drummer's notebook. 'I was going to look at this earlier, but we were having such a lovely tea party that it slipped my mind. As there's no sleep to be had at the moment, we'd better look at it now.'

Hettie returned to her chair with the sweets and Alice's little black book, while Tilly scrambled from her blanket and joined her on the arm of the chair. Flicking through the first few pages, it became clear that Alice used her Filofax to manage every part of her life: there was a page for each date, filled with diary entries and lots of notes, and a number of separate bits of paper were added to the pages or clipped in to keep them safe; these additions seemed to be snatches of poetry or half-written songs. 'She wasn't just a drummer, then,' Hettie said, sifting through the loose notes. 'Listen to this one. "Big shout, freak out, get out now. No way, throw away, final bow." Not the most hopeful set of lyrics I've ever heard, but she was fond of her rhythms and rhymes, that's for sure.'

Tilly picked up the book for a closer inspection of the diary, turning to the most recent entries. 'Look – this one's for last Friday. "Hacked off. D hardly said a word. Sick of pretending – all this not worth the hassle. PS not happy! Getting out as soon as this tour is over." That was the last thing she wrote.'

'Well, there was clearly something going on in the band. We witnessed that at rehearsals, but I wonder what she meant by "pretending"? And we need to find out more about the relationship between Alice and Deirdre, as there was clearly some sort of issue going on. Is that "PS" a postscript or does it refer to Patty Sniff?'

Tilly shrugged, flicking back through the pages until she came to the recording sessions at Tabby Road. 'She was obviously happy at this point. She writes: "Settling into the backing tracks, and S adding some great bass lines. P just brilliant. Meeting D after session for supper." So she's referring to Patty as P here, I think, and Deirdre is obviously still in favour.'

Hettie reached absent-mindedly for a liquorice allsort, but Tilly, when offered, waved the bag away, knowing she'd exceeded her limit. 'I think this Filofax may give us some answers,' said Hettie, picking an awkward piece of liquorice out of one of her side teeth with her claw. 'If Suzi or Deirdre was involved in Alice's murder, the good news is that the killing stops here. It could easily be a domestic situation within the band.'

'But murder is a bit extreme, isn't it?' Tilly objected.

'Not in the slightest,' said Hettie. 'I've often been tempted to murder band members – mostly drummers and bass players, it has to be said. Blood, egos and tempers run hot in bands – just remember you have to be thrown together to make music. Most bands are like a totally mismatched family, with individual agendas, crushed creativity and usually no money at the end of it.'

'But they were fantastic at rehearsals once they got going, and they all looked like they were enjoying it.'

'Ah, well, that's the point,' said Hettie. 'Most musicians will tell you that the only thing that glues a band together is that moment they all strive for, the performance – it's everything. You can have a full-scale catfight seconds before going on stage, but the moment the lights hit your face and the first chords are delivered, everything changes. When a band comes together, it's like walking on air. There's no feeling like it.'

Tilly knew that Hettie was speaking from experience, and the far-off look in her eyes told her that life on the road had been far from easy. She was beginning to understand why her friend had become so antisocial in her later years, and it made her realise how lucky she was to enjoy the bond which the two cats had formed together. She looked at the next page in the diary to see how supper had gone with Deirdre. 'Oh dear – look at this bit. "Fed up with this on–off thing. Really getting to me now, and she's moved into my space. Going solo could be a really cool thing to do. Great session today, and two more tracks laid down." I wonder what all that means?'

'It means that if we don't go to sleep soon, we'll be fit for nothing tomorrow,' said Hettie, yawning. 'We'll have to go through this Filofax page by page – a little light reading on the bus, I think, but we'll have to make sure no one sees it.'

'At least Patty won't be a problem there,' said Tilly, settling down on her blanket.

Chapter Twelve

Tilly woke to the roar of the Butters' bread ovens, which were situated just outside their room. Being at the back of a bakery was a drawback if you wanted a lie-in, although Hettie seemed to achieve one on most days. The Butter sisters were always up at four, making and baking enough pastries, breads and pies to fill their shop. Tilly had always been an early riser, too. In the days when she was homeless, she had found places to sleep out of the weather in shop doorways, old sheds and piles of leaves under hedges, but cats with homes could be cruel to strays and she had made a point of being up and moving on before the town came to life, for fear of being physically removed from her night's refuge. These days it was very different: she woke surrounded by the safety of their little room, knowing that she had plenty of time to coax her arthritic limbs into life before addressing the practicalities of each new day. The first job was always going to be waking Hettie as gently as possible; she'd learnt that the tone of each day was very much set by her frame of mind, and a rude awakening could be disastrous.

Staying on her blanket, Tilly reached for Alice Slap's Filofax. The clock on the staff sideboard said it was nearly five, and much too early to wake Hettie. Trying to go back to sleep was pointless, as she was too excited about the tour, but she was also keen to delve further into Alice's life, feeling as sure as Hettie that the answer to Alice's murder lay within her diary. She turned to the pages they'd been reading the night before, which described the sessions at Tabby Road. It was clear that Alice was enjoying recording Patty's album, as she'd written a number of complimentary notes about working with the star, but there was a curious melancholy that leapt off the pages as the sessions progressed; something had clearly happened between her and Deirdre. Later on, Tilly found what she thought was a very significant comment: 'Looks like the tour's on. Thinking of jumping ship now. I just can't face seeing D every day. She's really got it coming to her!' The next pages were blank, except for the odd appointment, and the diary didn't really pick up again until the last few days, which Tilly had already looked through.

She decided to go back to the beginning of the year to see if the animosity between Deirdre and Alice had been going on for some time. January was full of excitement, as it would appear that they were just forming The Cheese Triangles. Alice had much to say about her new bandmates, and all was positive and friendly. There was, however, a significant change by April, with a big announcement: 'Patty Sniff wants us to record her new album with her! Unbelievable!' The words were underlined in thick felt-tip pen, and there was another important comment: 'D has asked me to move in. S says it'll never work and could get in the way of the band.' Annoyingly, there were a number of blank pages that followed, where Alice had written nothing except the odd word, but she was obviously happy. 'Bliss!', 'Brilliant day!' and a whole page embellished with a highly decorated 'LOVE' and hearts soaring from the letters. Tilly was beginning to understand: it would appear that Alice's friendship with Deirdre had blossomed into something more than bandmates. Reading between the lines, the friendship had soured very quickly, but the two cats had found themselves caught up in the obligations of recording and the prospect of a tour – and the old adage applied: the show must go on. Keeping her assumptions in mind, Tilly made a random list of suspects, putting Deirdre Nightshade right at the top. Motive was obvious: Alice had become a nuisance and was threatening the band. She put Suzi Quake second on the list, then added the names of the rest of the touring party in no particular order, taking care to put Patty and Boobah at the bottom on the assumption that neither of them was physically capable of murdering anyone.

The clock had moved on by three hours, and Tilly knew that it was time to start the process of waking Hettie. An early start was bound to be a problem, but she'd taken the precaution of putting aside a couple of sausage rolls from their Sunday tea in the hope that they would act as a welcome stimulant to Hettie's mood. She folded up her blanket and put it in the staff sideboard, then padded across to the kettle.

Her plan of a calm and controlled awakening was scuppered by a loud thumping on the door, accompanied by the dulcet tones of Beryl Butter. 'Wakey-wakey, you two! I come bearing savouries and confectionery for your trip!'

Hettie struggled into the land of the living, sitting bolt upright in her chair with her hackles on end, as Tilly opened the door. Beryl held a tray piled high with white paper bags, and her sister stood a little behind with a stack of brown ones. 'White bags are sweet, brown bags are savoury!' boomed Beryl. 'Where would you like them?'

Tilly fetched the tartan shopper, which she'd parked by the filing cabinet. 'I thought the food might fit in here,' she said, relieving Beryl of the sweet parcels.

'Well, you'd better stick the savouries in first, as the sweets are a bit more delicate. Sister's baked a few extras to keep you going,' said Betty, helping Tilly to transfer the brown parcels to the shopper. 'Crisps are still to come, but you might want to choose your flavours in the shop.'

Betty turned on her heel and went back to the bakery, where a queue was already building outside the shop. Beryl loaded her white bags into the shopper and turned to the huge ovens, pulling out a dozen golden-brown steak pies. Tilly shut the door on this glorious scene, knowing that she would now have to deal with Hettie's rude awakening.

The rant was short and to the point. 'Is there no bloody peace to be found in this world? A cat can't even lay her head down without some early riser shouting the odds. They're a scourge on society. If cats started their days later, there'd be less time for trouble.'

'And fewer pies and pastries to eat,' replied Tilly, preparing the mugs for their tea. 'Look at my tartan shopper, full to bursting with lovely things – and Betty and Beryl were up so early to make all of them for us.'

Hettie was about to expand her thesis on early risers, but thought better of it. Tilly distracted her by placing a mug of milky tea and a sausage roll on the arm of her chair, then took her own breakfast to the desk where she'd gathered a few books which she wanted to take on tour with her. Books were very important to Tilly, especially crime fiction. It was her way of keeping up to date with the latest methods of investigation. She particularly enjoyed Agatha Crispy's Miss Marble cases, but had developed a real interest in Nicolette Upstart's books since meeting her at the town's literary festival. She was especially pleased to have Nicolette's latest book, *Nine Lives*, to take with her, and she'd chosen *The Moving Claw* from Miss Crispy to reread, even though she remembered which cat had done it.

Hettie downed her morning tea and demolished her sausage roll in seconds, then spent at least five minutes on cleaning her ears and face to make sure she looked fit for the day ahead. She stretched, and reluctantly left her chair to join Tilly at the desk.

Pleased to see that the sausage roll had calmed Hettie's temper, Tilly decided to update her friend on the revelations she'd discovered in Alice Slap's Filofax. Hettie listened to the diary entries as Tilly read them out, agreeing that Deirdre Nightshade had earned her rightful place as chief suspect. If Tilly was right, it was a simple case of extreme band politics, but there was one question that needed consideration. 'If Deirdre – or Deirdre and Suzi – murdered Alice, why would they want to endanger the tour?' asked Hettie. 'They couldn't have known that Cormac was a drummer, and as far as I can see, being on tour with Patty Sniff is a big break for The Cheese Triangles. Alice obviously thought so. Why didn't they wait until after the tour and then get rid of her? After all, it's only a few dates. What did Alice do or say to make them strike out now?'

That, of course, was just one of the questions that Hettie and Tilly would have to find an answer to, but the clock on the sideboard was heading rapidly for ten. The two tabbies busied themselves in gathering their final bits of packing together before hauling their luggage out into the hot sunshine to await the arrival of Psycho Derek's bus.

Chapter Thirteen

The bus arrived just as the St Kipper's church clock was striking ten. Poppa sprang from his seat to accommodate Hettie and Tilly's suitcase in the hold, which was already crammed with band gear. Tilly insisted on taking the tartan shopper and a small bag of paw luggage on board with her, announcing that the food would be having its own seat. Having driven the bus from the Fudges' driveway, Derek retreated to his own accommodation at the back of the vehicle and allowed Bruiser – who looked like he'd just woken up – to take his place at the steering wheel.

Within minutes of the bus's arrival, the town's postmistress, Lavender Stamp, appeared on the pavement, looking every bit the demented harridan. As far as Lavender was concerned, that particular bit of pavement belonged to her. She threw her paws up in the air and shouted every threat that she could muster, demanding that the bus be removed from the front of her post office immediately. Settling down in her seat, Hettie smiled and waved at the postmistress, knowing that her sarcasm would only serve to enhance Lavender's performance. The rest of the passengers started up a chant of 'Here we go, here we go', which drowned out Lavender's protestations – and, to make matters worse, Marley Toke's old army truck arrived and parked behind the bus, causing the postmistress to hyperventilate. It was lucky for her that Betty and Beryl had come out of the bakery to wave the tour off: seeing Lavender's distress as she collapsed on the pavement, Betty shot across the street and forced her to breathe into one of the bakery's paper bags. While the panic attack gradually subsided, Poppa had a quick word with Marley about the proposed route and leapt back on the bus to take his seat.

'Step on the gas and wipe that tear away!' cried Hettie in a rare public outburst of excitement. 'Summer of Fluff, here we come!' The tour party cheered as one, as the bus and Marley's truck pulled out into the High Street in convoy, heading for their first date at West Grunting Pavilion.

The tour party settled down into little cliques, as the bus gobbled up the miles. Derek and Belisha appeared to be having a bit of a row behind their curtain at the back of the bus; Cormac and Tarmac had settled down to discuss the week's horse racing fixtures, noting that there was plenty of Irish horse flesh on offer to put their money on; Enya and Kitty were engaged in writing postcards home; and Moya and Aisling were listening – not too intently – to Boobah's recollections of her days with the Bolshy Ballet Company, and how she'd defected to become principal dancer with the Dewesbury Hoofers, which was where she'd had her accident. Tilly was fascinated by Boobah's story as she eavesdropped on the conversation, and was dying to hear more about the accident, but Boobah fell asleep during the telling of her own story, leaving Moya and Aisling free to paint their claws a lurid green for the evening performance.

Only Patty sat alone, and Tilly felt for her, as she stared straight ahead at the seat in front, her dark glasses hiding her blindness. She wondered what that life must be like for the punk star, isolated and forced to trust cats she couldn't see, going to sleep in the dark and waking up in the dark, oblivious to unseen dangers. Hettie was deep in whispering conversation with Poppa, bringing him up to speed on Alice's murder, so it seemed the perfect moment for Tilly to get to know Patty a little better, especially as she had been given the job of talking to her about the night Alice died. She shuffled into the seat next to Patty, announcing her arrival. The singer seemed pleased to have some company and insisted on running her paws across Tilly's face by way of a proper introduction. 'Flat nose, long hair, and I bet you got some great stripes. Good whiskers, too.' Tilly was pleased with her appraisal, although the stripes were a little erratic, but the ice had been broken and Patty seemed keen to chat. 'You been on tour before?' she asked.

'No, it's my first time. I usually help my friend, Hettie Bagshot, with her detective agency,' Tilly explained, feeling a little shy as she talked about herself. 'We live behind the bakery in the town, and Poppa is an old friend of Hettie's from her music days. Actually, he's a plumber now, but you probably know that. Anyway, Poppa asked us to help with the tour, and as it's very hot and we're very bored because we didn't book a seaside holiday, we said yes.'

Patty looked across at Tilly as if she could see her. 'Hang on a minute – let's rewind. You say that Hettie Bagshot is on the tour? *The* Hettie Bagshot? I don't believe it! That's so cool. I've got all her albums. We did a few festivals together, but I never met her. I loved that folky stuff she did. Great stories, and much nastier than the stuff I was putting out. So, why isn't she still doing it?'

'I think she decided to stop while she was winning. I'm not sure she liked her bands very much,' Tilly said, not sure how far into Hettie's history she should go.

'Yeah, right – don't talk to me about bands,' said Patty, warming to her subject. 'I'd happily do without one if I could. I've often thought about going on with pre-recorded backing tracks, but I'm not sure the vibe would be the same. I make a point of steering clear of all my band except at gig time – can't stand any of them, especially this new lot, although I did like Alice. The other two are just out for what they can get and using me as their springboard.'

Tilly was taken aback at Patty's forthright attitude to her band, but felt that now would be a good moment to ask about Alice's death. 'It's such a shame that Alice had her accident. Did you say you heard her choking?'

'Well, it was all a bit weird, really. They'd all gone out to get some food and Alice said she'd bring me something, so I told her I'd have whatever she was having. I got meself a catnip roll-up together and just lay on me bed, chilling out. Then I heard this row going on outside – bit of a catfight, really. Alice was shouting something about getting her own back. I'm not sure who she was shouting at, but the next thing I heard was the front door slam and someone running up the stairs. It must have been Alice, because she came into our room and I knew she had food 'cause I could smell the bacon. I asked her what was up, and she said it was nothing she couldn't sort. She gave me me bacon sandwich and went out again. I must have fallen asleep for a bit. The next thing I knew, Alice was coughing. To be honest, I thought I was dreaming, but when Suzi and Deirdre came in later and started screaming, I realised that something had gone down. I wasn't even sure if it was morning at that point, and then the room started filling with cats, all carrying on. I sort of felt a bit invaded, you know – it was like I wasn't there. In the end, I shouted for someone to tell me what was happening and one of the Irish cats said that Alice had choked on a bacon sandwich. It was then I realised that the coughing I'd heard wasn't a dream, and I felt so bad. Maybe I could have saved her by thumping her on the back or something. What a waste of a good drummer.'

'When you heard the coughing, did you hear or smell anything else?' asked Tilly.

Patty shook her head. 'Not really. The whole room smelt of bacon… But come to think of it, there *was* a strong smell of Alice's perfume. Reeve Gosh, I think – not great with bacon. Why do you ask?'

Tilly had been caught out and was desperately trying to think of a reply to make her question sound harmless, when fate intervened and the bus lurched violently to one side, throwing all the passengers but Patty into the gangway. 'Bugger!' said Bruiser, amid the tangle of paws, tails and fur. 'I'm afraid we've got a blowout. All paws to the pump, and we should have it fixed in no time.'

Poppa disentangled himself from Hettie, who in turn had become buried under the tartan shopper, and made his way over a jumble of Irish dancers to the front of the bus, where – after removing Boobah from the door well – he managed to open the door. Bruiser followed him out of the bus and the two cats went in search of the spare. It was noticeable that Derek was keeping a low profile, and Bruiser soon discovered why: the spare tyre was nowhere to be found.

'Well, that really is a sod!' said Poppa, kicking the flat tyre. 'We've got at least thirty miles to go and not a garage in sight.'

Marley, who had executed the perfect emergency stop as the bus veered to one side, joined Poppa and Bruiser to stare at the offending tyre. 'Dat be a mighty bad dose of misfortune, I'd say. I got two spare tyres on me truck, but I don't suppose dem wheels will work on dis.'

'They might,' said Poppa, trying to remain positive. 'Where do you keep them?'

'Day on de top of me roof. I got me jack up dere as well.'

Poppa lost no time in springing up onto the roof of Marley's truck and choosing the better of the two tyres. He lowered it over the side to Bruiser's waiting paws, followed by the jack, and the two cats set about taking the burst tyre off the bus. By now, the tour party had recovered sufficiently to take the air and disembarked one by one, rubbing banged heads and bruised legs. Hettie was none the worse for her close call with the tartan shopper and Tilly had escaped injury altogether, but Belisha Beacon was making much of a slight nosebleed, and Enya had banged her paw rather badly and was receiving concerned sympathy from Kitty.

The make-or-break moment came when Poppa and Bruiser hauled Marley's spare wheel into place at the front of the bus. It seemed to fit, so Bruiser tightened the nuts with the wheel brace. 'Not perfect,' he said, standing back to look at his work, 'but it'll 'ave to do fer now till I can get to a garage. I'll 'ave to take it steady, so we'd better get on.'

Poppa returned the jack to Marley's truck and the cats all clambered back onto the bus, chatting about their narrow escape. The burst tyre seemed to have created a welcome unity amongst the entertainers, and all were relieved to be back on the road to West Grunting. The first gig of the tour was in sight – except for Patty, of course.

Chapter Fourteen

West Grunting Pavilion was perched on the cliff, just outside the town of the same name. It had been a very important venue for bands over the years, attracting many top names. Hettie's own band had played there on one of her album tours, but as Bruiser brought the tour bus to a standstill outside, she noted that the grandeur she'd experienced back then had rather faded. The building was in dire need of a lick of paint, and old posters still clung to the display boards at the entrance, flapping in the breeze coming off the sea. A flock of gulls was the only sign of life, gathered high up on the Pavilion's ornate façade.

Hettie followed Poppa off the bus, keen to stretch her legs, and the two cats stared in through the glass entrance doors, which were firmly locked. 'No one about yet, then,' said Hettie. 'Maybe there's someone round the back.'

Poppa was about to go and check when a short-haired ginger cat on a bicycle skidded to a halt by the bus. 'Sorry I'm late! I couldn't find the keys. You know how it is – you put them down and then can you find them again? Welcome to West Grunting Pavilion, one of the oldest and most celebrated concert halls on the North Norfolk coast. I'm Ronnie Shortcrust, but my friends call me Flaky.'

I bet they do, thought Hettie, as the ginger cat pulled an enormous bunch of keys out of his bicycle basket. 'I'll get the stage door open first so you can get your gear in. We don't have a green room as such, but we do have an orange room with a sink and a couple of sofas if the artists would like to hang out in there,' said Ronnie Shortcrust before disappearing round the back of the building. Poppa asked Bruiser to drive the bus closer to the stage door, and then directed Marley and her truck to a space where she could set up her field kitchen.

Hettie helped Bruiser with Boobah's ramp, and once the dancing mistress had rolled off the bus, the rest of the party followed. Tilly waited until last to lead Patty off, steering her through the stage door and out of harm's way, and leaving her contentedly perched on one of the flight cases in the wings. Poppa and Bruiser wasted no time in unloading the gear, placing the heavier equipment on a sack barrow which Poppa carried everywhere. The sack barrow had been with him longer than he could remember; it had been on all of Hettie's tours and was now an integral part of his plumbing business.

'At least the stage still looks the same,' said Hettie, as Tilly joined her for a look round. 'I was on a support tour the first time I played here, and there was a bit of a scuffle in the end. I bet Poppa remembers it – he got himself a sore ear that night.'

'Why? What happened?' asked Tilly.

'We'd just got our first big recording deal, and the record company put us on a tour to support this cat called Roy and his band. He was okay, but his roadies took against our lovely huge tour posters, which took up most of the foyer. They were really smart, with pictures of my new album in silver and black, and there was also a life-size cardboard cutout of me. Poor old Roy didn't have any posters, you see, so his roadies decided to even things up by taking our display boards and dumping them over the cliff into the sea. Poppa caught them at it, but he was outnumbered and took a nasty bite to his ear.'

'So it wasn't just the bands you had to worry about,' observed Tilly.

'No. Touring was so competitive – and the fans could be a real nuisance, too, stealing the song lists from the front of the stage before we'd even come on and getting us to sign them later so they could show off to their friends. Then there were the know-alls, who pinned you down about the verse you'd chosen to miss out of a particularly long folk ballad. Folk rock attracted the pedants, unfortunately.' Hettie lowered her voice to a whisper as Derek and Belisha pushed past with their magic box, hoping to place it centre stage, as they were the opening act. 'Anyway, how did you get on with Patty?'

Tilly looked round and decided that there were too many ears twitching to discuss her conversation with the singer. Flaky, Bruiser and Poppa were busy setting up the stage, and the Irish dance troupe was milling around doing stretching exercises. Suzi and Deirdre were sitting on their guitar cases, smoking catnip and waiting to be called for a soundcheck. 'I think we'd better see if our stuff's all right on the bus,' she suggested, nodding towards the stage door. Hettie followed her back onto the bus, where the two friends could speak freely without an audience. It was hot and stuffy, though, so Hettie decided that this might be a good moment to enjoy a spot of sea air and a parcel or two from the tartan shopper. Tilly was pleased at the prospect of a picnic and chose randomly from the white and brown paper bags. The two friends then headed for a peaceful spot on the cliff to enjoy their food and some sunshine, away from the chaos backstage.

Tilly recounted the conversation she'd had with Patty as Hettie lay back in the sun, having devoured a large cheese scone and a ring doughnut. Tilly's bags offered a ham roll and two jam tarts, which she was very pleased with, and she made a half-hearted attempt at brushing the pastry crumbs out of her fur while she waited for Hettie to respond.

Eventually, she did. 'It seems to me that things had obviously come to a head for Alice that night. There was clearly an ongoing row – we assume with Deirdre, but maybe with Suzi as well, as those two seem to stick together like glue. Alice was obviously keen on getting her own back over something. If you keep going with Patty, that would be good. Ask her how Alice got on with the other two; she might have confided in Patty about her feelings for Deirdre. I'll see if I can get Deirdre to talk about Alice. It's strange, you know, but no one seems particularly upset by Alice's death.'

'On a different subject altogether, Patty is a big fan of yours. She told me she has all your albums, and she couldn't believe you were on the tour. She called you *THE* Hettie Bagshot. I think you might get more out of her if you chewed over old times together.'

Hettie felt quite puffed up at the thought of a big star like Patty Sniff having her albums; there was obviously more to Patty's musical tastes than hissing and spitting. 'It's very odd,' she said, 'but I actually keep forgetting that Patty is blind. She may get lost occasionally in new surroundings, but she does seem to be fairly together.'

'And she's very nice,' added Tilly. 'I wonder if she's always been blind?'

'The story goes that it happened when a lighting rig fell on her during a school play,' Hettie said. 'It was one of those Greek ones, where mother cats kill their kittens and eat them in a pie, then everyone gets shipwrecked on some volcanic island where they're turned into mutant cats. I read about it in one of the music papers. Patty got a big compensation payout from the school and set up her first band with one of her school friends, Anthrax Lunachick. She split from Patty after the first few hits and went on to be huge on the punk circuit in her own right, before electrocuting herself on her curling tongs.'

'These punk cats don't have much luck, do they?' said Tilly. 'At least Patty's still standing, even if she can't see. I suppose I'd better get back to her before she falls off the flight case.'

Hettie collected the empty paper bags and the two cats headed back to the Pavilion, noting that the car park at the back of the venue was filled with the smell of one of Marley's curry dishes. She'd opened the side of her truck and was busy stirring a giant vat of something delicious, as she prepared supper for the tour party. Next to the pot of curry was a baking tray filled with what Tilly liked to call 'Indian turnovers'; the golden-brown samosas had just come out of the oven and glistened in the hot sunshine.

When Hettie and Tilly reached the stage door, Bruiser was coming out with Ronnie Shortcrust. 'They're about to do a soundcheck, so I thought I'd slope off an' get this tyre sorted. Flaky 'ere is gonna show me where the local garage is.' Flaky seemed pleased to be on a mission and offered a beaming smile as he followed Bruiser onto the bus.

Patty was still sitting on the flight case where Tilly had parked her, but Suzi, Deirdre and Cormac were on stage, putting the finishing touches to their individual set-ups. Poppa was down the hall, in the centre with the mixing desk, and brought the musicians to order. 'Right-o, mateys! Let's have some drums to start with,' he shouted. 'Give us a bit of snare and then hit the tom-toms for me, Cormac.'

The Irish cat responded, and Poppa adjusted the faders on the mixing desk until he was happy with the drum sound. 'Okay, Suzi, let's have some bass. I think you'll need to turn your stack down a bit. Yep, that's nice. Now, Deirdre, a bit of a solo from you, please.'

Deirdre Nightshade launched into a screaming guitar solo which made even Patty put her paws over her ears. Poppa shouted at her to turn down her stage amplifier, but for obvious reasons she couldn't hear. Suzi crossed the stage and pulled the guitarist's lead out to silence her. 'What the hell do you think you're doing!' Deirdre screamed. 'Try that again and you'll have all six of these machine heads in your face.' She advanced towards Suzi, pushing her guitar towards the bass player in a jousting movement.

The show on stage was probably the best one on the whole tour, and the entertainers not involved watched in fascination as the two punk cats faced up to each other, slowly circling and ready to pounce. Cormac sank behind Alice's drum kit, hoping that the catfight wouldn't come his way, while Poppa strode to the front of the stage, keen to avert any damage to the instruments or equipment. 'Come on, girls – leave it out. We've got a show to put on. Why not take five to cool off while I check out Patty's vocals?'

The two musicians continued to eye each other up, but Poppa had broken the tension. Suzi backed off first and left the stage, heading for the car park. Deirdre glared after her, before spitting out a whole row of expletives which she felt were fit for purpose. She then slammed her guitar down, leaving the stage in the opposite direction to find solace in the orange room that Flaky had recommended.

'Not a bad start to day one of the tour,' said Hettie. 'Things can only get worse.'

Tilly giggled nervously. Leaving Hettie and Poppa at the mixing desk, she helped Patty to centre stage, where the punk star proceeded to test her microphone by reciting Mr Wilco Wordsmith's poem, 'Daffodils', much to the amazement of any onlookers, who had expected something a little harder-edged. Suzi Quake returned to the stage, swiftly followed by Deirdre, and – as if nothing had happened – the band played the introduction to 'Sausage and Slash', the title track to Patty's new album. Patty moved close to her microphone to bring in the first verse while Cormac pounded out the beat, and as the music took over, there was nothing but respect and mutual appreciation from the performers on stage.

When Patty and Poppa were happy with the sound, it was time for Kitty O'Shea and her dancers to be put through their paces – much to the annoyance of Belisha, who was keen for Magical Mystery Paws to go next. 'Them dancers 'ave been bobbin' up and down since we got off the bus,' she said loudly into Poppa's ear. 'They don't need any more practice. Derek 'asn't quite perfected 'is act yet, an' we need the time more than that Irish lot of bouncin' tabards.'

Poppa was about to reply, but Boobah saved him the effort by aiming her wheelchair at Belisha, stopping just short of her white plastic boots. 'You vud do vell to keep your insults to yourselv. My dancers do not do ze bob or ze bounce, and cats like you belong in ze salt mines.' The insult was too profound for Belisha, and Derek brought the altercation to an end by dragging her away before any further harm was done, clearly rueing the day that he'd snatched her away from her zebra crossing.

Enya was first on stage, setting up her small keyboard in front of the drum kit. Poppa encouraged her to play something to help him balance the sound, expecting a medley of Irish dance tunes, but Enya amazed everyone by launching into one of her own compositions: a beautiful, ethereal soundscape which she'd cobbled together while serving green beer in her father's Donegal tavern. She'd called the piece 'Caribbean Boot' and hoped one day to make an album full of similar works.

'She's very good, isn't she?' said Tilly.

'Yes, she is. Goodness knows what she's doing messing about with Kitty's troupe,' observed Hettie. 'She could be a star in her own right.'

Boobah had clearly overheard their comments and clapped her paws, keen to bring the recital to an end. She knew in her heart that Enya was too good for banging out Irish jigs, but that was what was needed, so Enya's true talent had to be suppressed or confined to her own bedroom, where no one was listening. Allowing her to develop into other areas of music would endanger the very existence of the dance troupe, and that was a risk which Boobah simply refused to take.

When Poppa was happy with the keyboard sound, the dancers took to the wings and started bobbing up and down. One by one, they moved across the stage in a long line, led by Kitty O'Shea, and began a series of synchronised step dances. To break the monotony, Boobah shouted, 'Taps!' and the troupe bobbed back to the side of the stage, where they quickly swapped their dancing shoes for little boots. The performance went up a level as they returned with a fine display of tap dancing, and Cormac broke the line to give an impressive solo, leaping and twisting as he hammered out the rhythm with his feet.

Boobah was pleased but tried not to show it, pointing out that Kitty had been a little late changing into her tap shoes and telling Moya that she needed to blow her nose before she started, as handkerchiefs were not part of their stage clothes. The dance troupe filed out into the late afternoon sunshine, just in time to see Bruiser and Flaky arriving back in Derek's bus, which now sported a new tyre and a spare.

Marley had put out a few picnic chairs around her food truck and a small café society was beginning to form. Patty had found her way across the car park by following the smell of Marley's curry, and Suzi and Deirdre joined her for a rare bit of band camaraderie. The dancers – hungry after their onstage workout – joined the musicians, and Marley handed out freshly baked naan bread as a starter to the main event.

Hettie and Tilly stayed with Poppa in the hall, keen to witness Magical Mystery Paws in rehearsal. On Belisha's instructions, Derek had been to Jessie's charity shop and bought himself a rather dated gold lamé suit, which had originally belonged to Spiro Belch, the town's bingo caller. Spiro had dropped dead in the middle of a session – much to the annoyance of Elsie Haddock, who was only one number short of a line – and Jessie had been pleased to get rid of the suit; these days, there was very little call for gold lamé.

'This is going to be worth watching,' said Poppa. Derek and Belisha appeared on stage, dragging the magic box and a black foldaway card table, which Belisha piled high with cards, egg cups, silk handkerchiefs and a top hat containing a stuffed white rabbit. As Flaky pulled up the red-and-blue spots in the lighting box at the back of the hall, the stage came to life and the magic box sparkled impressively along with Derek's suit. Belisha looked ridiculous in a bright red, low-cut evening gown that had clearly been made for a taller cat. She danced around Derek, emphasising the tricks that he hadn't yet performed.

'Could you test your mic, Derek mate?' shouted Poppa.

''Ee's not Derek at the moment!' Belisha bellowed from the stage. ''Ee's got to be in the zone. 'Ee's Magical Mystery Paws!'

'I don't actually give a sod who he is or which zone he's in. I just need him to check that mic!' replied Poppa, who was keen to sample Marley's curry before the audience arrived. Derek responded by counting to ten into the microphone. 'Okay, that'll do. Take it away!'

Derek froze, staring out into the empty auditorium. 'I don't think I can do this,' he said. 'I'm not a magician. I'm just a cat who paints buses.'

'Don't be ridiculous!' screamed Belisha. 'It's your big chance to be famous. Just get on with it – do the disappearing trick.'

The look on Derek's face made it clear that he would love to disappear, but that wasn't quite what Belisha meant. He moved towards the magic box and invited his assistant to step inside, forgetting to put the microphone up to his mouth. Belisha made much of cramming herself into the space before Derek shut the door on her. He moved round the box, mumbling and striking it with his magic wand before opening the door with a flourish. The trick worked. Belisha was nowhere to be seen, much to the relief of Poppa, Hettie and Tilly – for a variety of reasons. Derek seemed as surprised as they were that the trick had been successful and shut the door again, intending to bring Belisha back but she pre-empted him by appearing from behind the box and giving the lie to the magic. Disappointed and a little angry, Derek moved on to the knife trick, forcing Belisha back into the box and stabbing six knives into the slits in the door.

Tilly held her breath, as Derek circled the box again, tapping it with his wand before withdrawing the knives. It was Belisha who pushed the door open this time, making much of the fact that she was still in the land of the living and without a scratch. 'I think that will do for now,' said Poppa, 'but you'll have to get used to using the mic, Derek mate, or the audience won't know what's going on.' Belisha was about to play the Magical Mystery Paws card again, but Poppa, Hettie and Tilly headed swiftly for the door, making it clear that they had zoned out.

Chapter Fifteen

Marley Toke's catering was certainly the highlight of the day so far. Her chicken curry, samosas and freshly fried poppadoms united almost the whole touring party with a congenial meal in the sun; only Derek and Belisha collected their food and scuttled back to the bus with it.

Ronnie Shortcrust invited himself to the pre-show supper and enthralled the gathering with his infinite knowledge of West Grunting and its heroes, much to the delight of Tilly, who loved a good story. 'Time's ticking on, but I'll tell you one more before I go and open the box office,' he said as Marley joined them, hot from her cooking. 'This story concerns a certain cat called Jammy Dodge, who resided in West Grunting in the early 1800s. Now, he was the local blacksmith and a renowned bare-paw prize fighter. The story goes that Jammy had a badly infected toe – gangrenous it was – and he was worried about it spreading and killing him, so he took himself off to his forge, rested his foot on the anvil, and with one mighty blow with his hammer and chisel, he chopped the infected toe off.'

The touring party gasped as one. Moya and Aisling pushed their paws into their mouths in horror, as Flaky continued his gratuitous tale, pleased to have a captive audience. 'The blood was everywhere, and Jammy knew he'd have to do something to stop its flow. He took up a red-hot poker from the fire and plunged it into the wound, where it sizzled the flesh and stopped the bleeding. Cauterisation, they call it.'

Flaky paused while Enya went to be sick at the back of Marley's truck. She'd never been able to cope with violence of any kind, and was particularly sensitive about paws. After Marley had mopped her up with a tissue, she returned to hear the happy ending to Flaky's story. 'Days later, the stump had healed completely and within weeks he was back fighting again – he did that until his death at the age of eighty-two. His blacksmith business boomed, too, as he was called in to cauterise wounds as far as Felix Toe. Right along the coast he went with his poker. Mind you, looking on the darker side, some of the cats he treated died of shock because the pain was unbearable, but he was trusted to do his best.'

'What did he die of?' asked Tilly.

'Old age, I think, although some say he fell into his own fire while he was cooking his tea at the forge.'

'Hoisted on his own tabard then,' said Tarmac, receiving peals of laughter for his joke.

Flaky had kept his audience well and truly amused with lurid stories of West Grunting, but now it was the tour party's turn to entertain a paying audience, starting with Magical Mystery Paws. Back on the bus, Derek was fast becoming Magical *Misery* Paws, thanks to another demoralising tirade from Belisha. She was shouting so loudly that she didn't hear Tilly climbing aboard – but Tilly heard plenty of what Belisha had to say. 'Pull yourself together, Derek! You need to forget all that other stuff and move on. Sittin' there sobbin' isn't helpin'. Look at all I've done for you and all them plans we made. When we get back off this tour, we're goin' to find a proper place instead of livin' in this tin can.'

Derek blew his nose and spoke. 'The thing is, Belisha, I love my bus. I don't want to live anywhere else, and I don't think I want to be Magical Mystery Paws. I just want to paint. I've spent years trying to be famous, and look where that's got me.'

Tilly crept into her seat, not wanting to be caught loitering in the gangway should Belisha suddenly appear through the curtain. The row continued, and this time it was Belisha who offered some home truths. 'How dare you sit there and tell me that me dream is over! I'm not livin' on a bus for the rest of me days while you fiddle about with a box of paints. Your pictures are rubbish. Just because you got that commisshin you seem to think you can paint anythin', and look how that turned out – unfinished, just like everythin' else you start.'

Derek began to sob again. Belisha sprang out from behind the curtain and flounced off the bus, not noticing Tilly, who was pretending to look for something under the seat. The sobs got louder, and Tilly wondered whether she should try to comfort him. She was about to call out to him when Deirdre Nightshade appeared. 'Poppa says you're stage gear?'

Tilly had quite forgotten her role of being in charge of stage clothes. 'Yes, that's right. How can I help?'

Deirdre looked towards the back of the bus, where Derek was still howling. 'What's going on with him?

Belisha stopped his pocket money or something? Why he took up with her, I'll never know. He don't know which side his bread's buttered, that one. Anyway, I got this rip in my favourite stage top. My fault – I caught it on something the other night. Shouldn't have worn it to go out in, really. Can you fix it?'

Tilly stared at the black T-shirt, realising that her qualifications for a job in the costume department were just as tenuous as Derek's charade with Magical Mystery Paws. The lighter, homely crafts like sewing had passed her by; faced with Deirdre's request, she was going to have to own up. 'I'm afraid my arthritis has affected my sewing,' she said. 'Maybe one of the dancers could help.'

'Sewing! I don't want it sewn up. I just need a safety pin – that'll look brilliant under the lights. The bigger the better.'

Tilly breathed a sigh of relief and burrowed to the bottom of the bag of bits and bobs that she'd packed for the tour. She pulled out an old toffee tin full of what she regarded as essentials and shook its content out onto the seat. There was string, a small magnifying glass, which she'd got in a cracker at Christmas, a miniature screwdriver set, claw clippers, a tin of Fishercat's Friends, a tube of glue and a chain of large safety pins clipped together.

'There you are,' she said, unclipping the biggest one. She offered it to Deirdre, who immediately hooked it into place across the rip in her stage top.

'Brilliant!' she said. 'I could sell that for twice the price I paid for it now. Alice had a shirt similar to this, except she had zips in hers – really smart!'

Tilly took her opportunity, as Deirdre had raised the subject of Alice without any prompting. 'You must be very sad about Alice,' she said. 'I expect you were good friends, being in a band together?'

'Yeah, she was an all right cat. Big temper, but she'd work that out on her drum kit. Drummers are strange creatures, really – all posturing and bluster. Deep down she was as lost as the rest of us.'

'Why was that?' said Tilly.

'Well, this music business takes no prisoners. It's all or nothing – no time for a proper life, love and that, or even someone to go home to at the end of a tour.'

'And is that what Alice wanted?'

'To be honest, I've no idea what she wanted. I make a point of not getting too involved with anyone. Gives me claustrophobia, having clingy stuff going on. Free is the only way to be. At least Alice has got that now, whether she wanted it or not.'

Their conversation was brought to an end by Derek, who appeared from behind the curtain looking dishevelled and puffy-eyed. He made his way down the bus and outside without saying a word to Tilly or Deirdre. Deirdre grabbed a bag from her seat and followed him, intent on bagging a corner of the orange dressing room to put her make-up on ready for the gig.

Tilly was left alone on the bus and decided, out of curiosity, to poke her nose behind the curtain at the back, where Derek and Belisha jealously guarded their space. To say it was a mess was an understatement: clothes were strewn everywhere, two plates of Marley's half-eaten curry congealed in the heat and an unmade bed had the contents of Belisha's make-up bag tipped out across it. Beneath the rear window there was a stack of canvasses and it was these that Tilly made a beeline for, having overheard Belisha's critique of Derek's art. The paintings, like the bus, were colourful and wild, and bold brushstrokes spoke of a confidence which was a far cry from the shambling wreck that Derek had become. The painting pushed to the back of the pile was unfinished; in fact, it was barely started, but was still recognisable as a portrait rather than pop art. The outline was sketched in light pencil, and it was clearly a cat posing on a day bed and surrounded by cushions. Derek had started to paint in the background, but the figure had no features. Tilly heard a noise behind her and hurriedly pushed the paintings back where she had found them, waiting expectantly for Belisha to burst through the curtain at any minute.

'Are you on here?' called a familiar voice. 'Patty needs some help to get ready, so I said I'd come and find you.'

Tilly appeared through the curtain, relieved to see Hettie. 'I've been eavesdropping and talking to Deirdre about Alice.'

'And?' said Hettie. 'Any revelations?'

'Well, Derek's in bits. Belisha is being really unkind to him, and this Magical Mystery Paws thing is all her idea – he just wants to paint. I've seen some of his paintings and they're much more cheerful than he is. I think he must have done them before he met her. There's a portrait he started, which I think was a commission, but it's hard to tell who it is as there aren't any features. The cat could be male or female, I suppose.'

'So that's Derek and his art. What about Deirdre and Alice? Any joy there?' demanded Hettie, a little impatiently.

'Not really. I don't think it lasted long – if there *was* anything between them at all. She did say that she doesn't like cats being clingy and wanted to be free, suggesting that Alice may not have agreed with her. She also said Alice was free now.'

'I suppose that depends on which way you look at it. I think we need to talk to Suzi next, if we get a chance, but it's nearly show time. I assume Derek and Belisha are waiting in the wings. The audience, for want of a better word, is just starting to arrive. They look like some sort of civilisation after a nuclear attack: clothes hanging off them in shreds, painted claws, safety pins, more body piercings than there are holes in a tea bag. They've obviously come to see Patty. Let's just hope there's not a riot when Magical Mystery bloody Paws comes on, hotly followed by the hoofers from Donegal!'

As it turned out, the West Grunting Pavilion audience was spared the excitement of Magical Mystery Paws and his not-so-glamorous assistant. By the time the lights went up, they were nowhere to be found, much to the delight of Boobah, who suggested to Poppa that her dancers could fill the void. Poppa was grateful for the offer, but had a better idea. 'A bit more dancing would be great,' he said tactfully, 'but I've decided to put Enya on solo to start us off.'

Boobah was horrified and said so, but her protestations fell on deaf ears, as Poppa encouraged the young Irish cat onto the stage for her debut solo performance. Patty, Deirdre, Suzi and Kitty's dance troupe all gathered in the wings to give her moral support, as she shyly put her keyboard through its paces, gaining more confidence as the hall filled with cats keen to see where the music was coming from.

Most of the audience had already decided to give Magical Mystery Paws a miss, preferring to hang out in the evening sunshine until Patty came on, but when word got round that the magic act wasn't happening, the cats wandered in to see what the alternative was. It wasn't their sort of music but most of them stayed, sucked in by Enya's haunting themes, which went down very well with the abundance of catnip being smoked.

Strangely enough, Boobah was the one doing the head-banging in the orange dressing room, more out of rage than in response to the music. She lived for her dancers, and Enya's talent was disruptive. It was bad enough that Cormac had become an honorary Cheese Triangle, without Enya striking out. Something would have to be done.

Enya finished her performance with 'Caribbean Boot' and brought the house down. Flaky, who was the self-appointed MC for the evening, had some trouble in announcing the interval, as the audience was baying for more, but Poppa had left the mixing desk to sell records on the merchandise stall, and Enya needed a glass of Ribena before she came back on with the dancers.

There was a crush in the foyer for Patty's albums and T-shirts. Poppa was pleased, as he'd gambled on the sales by investing his own money in the stock. Hettie joined him at the merch table, and together they emptied several boxes. It was good to see the Summer of Fluff Tour T-shirts hastily replacing some of the fashions that had turned up at the gig, and the audience seemed keen to fly the flag. Poppa had shrewdly asked Dorcas Ink to print a life-size portrait of Patty's face on the back, and the fans gobbled them up.

With Enya refreshed, Kitty O'Shea's Irish dance troupe took to the stage and put on a breathtaking performance, giving those watching an opportunity to practise their pogo skills ready for when Patty came on. Enya's earlier performance had prepared the ground for the dancers, who were being very well received, and Poppa couldn't help but feel that Magical Mystery Paws's no-show had played perfectly into his paws – or, more importantly, into the pockets of the roadie shorts that were now stuffed with money from his merch stall. The concert was going well, and – with the main act still to come – he expected album sales to go through the Pavilion's roof by the end of the night, especially if he could get Patty to do a signing in the car park later. The way things were looking, they might even make some money out of the tour after all.

Chapter Sixteen

Tilly was excited to be allowed into the orange room while Patty and her band prepared for their gig. Patty had insisted on it, as Tilly was turning into a half-decent minder who could be trusted to steer her away from the regular banana skins that blighted a life on tour.

Deirdre had changed into her safety-pinned black T-shirt, and was admiring herself in a cracked and rusted mirror, while Suzi looked on, clearly jealous of the makeover. 'I'm gonna need some new gear after this tour,' she said. 'Alice had some really good stuff. I should have borrowed some of it. I'm sure she wouldn't have minded.'

'You are joking, aren't you?' Deirdre responded peevishly. 'Fact is, she never liked you – and if you're honest, you couldn't stand her either. Why would you think you could borrow stuff from her?'

'Well, she doesn't need it where she's gone. I suppose her sister will just chuck it all in the bin when she comes to pick her stuff up. You're right about not liking her, though – too many distractions outside the band. You never knew whether she was staying or going.'

Patty looked up, signalling that she was about to enter the conversation. 'The point about Alice was that she was a brilliant drummer. If you'd both been kinder to her, she might have felt more *part* of the band. She was fine with me. We had some nice times together.'

'Only because she was sucking up to you. It was always Patty this and Patty that,' said Suzi, pulling on her Doc Martens.

Patty turned in Suzi's direction. 'I think you'd call that loyalty, although I doubt you'd recognise it. I know all about your plans to form your own band after this tour. I might be blind, but I can see where you two are coming from. You forget how long I've been in this business and the creeps I've shared a stage with.'

Tilly – who'd been sitting quietly, trying to make sense of the latest rows of Patty's tour knitting – resisted a strong urge to applaud the punk star for putting Suzi and Deirdre in their places. Deirdre, stung by Patty's remarks, grabbed her guitar and left the room, preferring to wait in the wings rather than share any more time with her band. Realising that she had some fences to mend with Patty, Suzi adopted a more conciliatory stance. 'It was only talk about forming a band, Patty. I love playing your stuff, and working in Tabby Road on the album was just the best gig I ever had. It's bad to speak ill of the dead, but Alice was very two-faced and she played us one against the other. I know she'd been through some stuff, but she was a real manipulator when she couldn't get her own way.'

'And you're not?' replied Patty.

Suzi was about to protest when the door was barged open by Boobah and her wheelchair, swiftly followed by Kitty's dancers, all hot and bothered from their performance. It was time for the main act and Cormac threw himself into a corner. He pulled off his green tabard, replacing it with a punk leather jacket, and ruffled the fur on the top of his head to give himself a just-fallen-out-of-bed look. Tilly was impressed with the transformation and shyly told him so. Knowing that her fence-mending with Patty had timed out, Suzi pulled her bass from its case and left the room.

'How am I looking?' asked Patty, feeling for Tilly's paw.

'Better than your knitting. I'm afraid I've had to unpick a lot of it. Shall I take you to the stage now?'

'Yeah, let's go and do some damage to their eardrums. Have we got our little Irish drummer with us?'

'All present, to be sure, and completely correct,' Cormac said, picking up his sticks as Boobah made several uncomplimentary comments under her breath. He led the way to the stage, followed by Tilly and Patty. Deirdre and Suzi were already there, checking their tuning, as the audience drifted back into the hall, refreshed by the small bar in the foyer and keen not to miss a note from the main event.

Flaky, who seemed to have made a lifelong friend of Bruiser in the few short hours they'd known each other, had run through the opening lighting sequence with him. Flaky was determined not to miss his big moment in bringing Patty on, and Bruiser had become the perfect secondary lighting technician, taking to the faders as if he'd been born to it. When the stage was set, Flaky signalled to Bruiser to bring up the followspot, and Cormac and Suzi immediately launched into the opening bars of 'Sausage and Slash'. The gig was underway and Flaky had missed his chance to do the introductions. Deirdre hit the first set of screeching chords, turning into her amp for extra feedback. With a little help from Tilly, Patty took to the stage and ripped the microphone from its stand, setting out her stall to a rapturous audience as the dry ice machine pumped its smoke across the band.

Tilly only felt the throb of absolute power briefly, as she led Patty to the centre of the stage, but it was enough for her to realise that the drug of performance was a dangerous one. As Patty worked the crowd, her blindness fell away like some biblical miracle, and Tilly really understood how hard it must have been for Hettie to give up her music.

Hettie was with Poppa at the mixing desk – the best seat in the house and a place she'd never been able to enjoy in her music days, when she was always on stage. Surprisingly, having heard snatches of Patty's new album during rehearsals and seen the songs performed live, she was developing a real appreciation for the punk star's music. There was a maturity about it which hadn't existed in the bad old days, when the new wave had lashed at Hettie's door, drowning everything she had achieved in out-of-tune guitars and violent rhetoric. It was clearly a new dawn for Patty Sniff, and Hettie didn't begrudge her any of it.

As Patty reached her penultimate number, the crowd's appreciation went up another level. Knowing that their time with her was coming to an end, the fans pogoed, clapped and cheered, raising their paws in salute to a star whose comeback they'd waited so long for. Hettie observed that the fans had grown old with their idol; there was no longer the insolence of youth – just a bunch of cats now battle-scarred from life and taking a break from normality to relive days that were never numbered.

Several encores later, Patty finally left the stage. Flaky, rather stupidly, made an attempt to wish the crowd a safe journey home, wanting to make his presence felt after being robbed of his introductions, but they pelted him with empty fizzy drinks cans. Dejected, he turned to winding up the wires at the back of the stage instead. Poppa unplugged the mixing desk and put it in its flight case before rushing out to the foyer to help Hettie on the merch table. She was under siege for copies of Patty's new album and had to send Bruiser back to the bus for more stock. Marley, who'd been watching from the back of the hall, took over the T-shirt sales, directing the queue out to the car park to relieve the crush inside.

'I was going to ask Patty to do a signing,' Poppa shouted into Hettie's ear, 'but she'll be mobbed if she tries. This lot are relentless.'

'We should get her to pre-sign some albums for tomorrow night,' suggested Hettie, ever on the lookout for a lucrative opportunity. 'Then we can charge extra for special copies.'

'Brilliant!' said Poppa, stuffing more notes into his pockets. 'That's if we've got any left to sell by then.'

The audience began going home: everyone was happy, wearing tour T-shirts and clutching copies of *Sausage and Slash*. Patty had collapsed on one of the orange room's sofas after her triumph, and it was a shame that she couldn't see the contrite look on Suzi's and Deirdre's faces as they quietly padded round the dressing room. It was crystal clear that unless they stuck with Patty, they would never achieve the adoration that had just washed over them out on stage; their big worry now was whether Patty would want to stick with *them*. After all, she held the cards even if she couldn't see them.

Making sure that her charge was safely back in the orange room, Tilly set out to find Hettie. She tried to get through the crowds in the foyer, but gave up as the crush was too much for her; instead, she joined Marley in the car park and lent a paw to the T-shirt sales. As Marley stuffed money into her substantial apron pockets, Tilly handed out the shirts until every customer had been served.

Back in the hall there was still much to do. Hettie remembered that the taking down and packing up at a gig was just about the worst moment on tour. She had done it with Poppa many times, and as she wound the wires round her paws and folded up the microphone stands, it all came flooding back to her. It was a thankless task, when all she really wanted to do was get back on the bus and relax with some of Betty and Beryl's paper bags for company. Bruiser was a great help and took on all the heavy lifting with Poppa, but that left Hettie with the fiddly bits, so she was pleased when Tilly turned up to help.

The two cats were tired. It had been a long day, and as they stared at the mass of wires still to coil, it was Hettie who voiced her thoughts. 'I don't know how I managed to do this every night for months on end,' she said. 'The gig bit was great, but it's all the stuff around it: travelling with cats you have nothing in common with except the music, all the different venues – some with stairs to cart the gear up, some with lifts that don't work – big stages, small stages and sometimes no stage at all. Then there's this bit – like clearing up after a party that's got out of hand, and knowing in your heart that it's going to be the same tomorrow and the next day.'

Tilly could see that Hettie was having one of her moments and decided to cheer her up by changing the subject. 'I wonder what happened to Derek and Belisha?' she said. 'It must be something serious for them not to do their act.'

Hettie had quite forgotten about Magical Mystery Paws; Enya had been such a success as the warm-up that Derek's no-show was a blessing. 'I suppose they'll come crawling back after we've finished all this packing up,' she said, 'but if I was Poppa, I'd pull the plug on the pair of them. From what you overheard, Derek's heart's not in it anyway, and don't even get me started on Belisha.'

Tilly giggled at what Hettie might have gone on to say, but made her own point. 'The trouble is, we're stuck with them because it's Derek's bus *and* his home.'

As things turned out, by the time everything was packed away and the tour party had clambered back on the bus, Belisha Beacon was no longer an issue – which brought a wave of relief to everyone, including Derek.

Chapter Seventeen

Flaky had given permission for the bus to spend the night in the Pavilion's car park, and the journey the following day would be a short one, as the next stop was the Palace Cinema in Felix Toe. The venue had stopped showing films after the projectionist caught his paw in the loading mechanism, which caused the screening of *Easy Rider* – a catnip-fuelled motorbike epic – to come to a sticky end long before its time. It had been decided to turn the venue over to the live music circuit until the projectionist's paw healed, but the change of use hadn't been welcomed by the good cats of Felix Toe. Poppa knew at the time of booking that the Palace could be the duff gig of the tour, although so far he'd kept that knowledge to himself.

The West Grunting Pavilion date had been a storming success, and after Flaky had settled up the door takings, Poppa, Hettie and Tilly spent some time counting the money from their night's work, adding in the album and T-shirt sales. Poppa was able to pay himself back for the merchandise *and* turn a healthy profit to go towards paying his entertainers and tour personnel. After sorting out the finances and waving Flaky off on his bicycle, the three friends boarded the bus, hoping for a light supper from Tilly's tartan shopper and some sleep – but, in the true tradition of touring, that simply wasn't going to happen. Bruiser was the only cat on the bus who was asleep. The rest of the company, including Boobah, was in party mode. Derek had come out from behind his curtain, and he and Tarmac – armed with their acoustic guitars – were offering accompaniment to the tour party's rousing chorus of 'All You Need is Fluff'.

Tilly scoured the seats, looking for Belisha, but she was nowhere to be found, which was just as well, as Suzi Quake had draped herself round Derek's neck as he strummed his guitar. Poppa waited until the final chorus had been sung before beckoning Derek over to his seat, keen to find out why Magical Mystery Paws had taken the evening off. Derek hung his head in apology as Tarmac launched into 'The Wild Rover'. Tilly couldn't resist joining in, but Hettie moved closer to Poppa and Derek, keen to hear what Derek had to say for himself.

'The thing is,' Derek began, 'Belisha has left me. It just wasn't working. We had a big bust-up earlier and she ran off, so I went after her. We walked along the clifftop for ages and she just kept shouting. In the end, I couldn't take any more. She said she wanted me to chuck everyone off the bus and drive her home or she'd leave me, so I told her that was okay with me. Truth is, I never wanted her to live on the bus anyway – she sort of moved in on me and turned my life upside down. I'm not good at relationships. I get all mixed up and can't decide what I want. Belisha took over everything, and I let her. We parted on the cliff and I carried on walking. When I got back to the bus, all her stuff was gone and I suddenly felt relieved that it was all over. I'm really sorry about letting you down with the magic act, but it was Belisha's idea and she convinced me it could work. I don't know what more I can say.'

Poppa patted Derek on his shoulder. 'No worries, mate – these things happen. Tour bust-ups are all par for the course, and I reckon you're well rid of her. As for Magical Mystery Paws, you're on the poster – but if you don't fancy doing the whole thing on stage, maybe you could keep the punters happy with a few tricks in the foyer as they come in? That thing you do with the magic box is cool, especially the knives.'

Derek brightened up. 'Well, I *could* do something like that, but I'd need an assistant.'

The singing had stopped and Suzi Quake caught Derek's last comment. 'How about me?' she suggested, making her way over. 'I'd love to get in your box.'

Derek wriggled uncomfortably, as Suzi threw her arms round his neck again. Hettie stared in amazement, wondering what it was about Psycho Derek that made him so attractive to certain female cats. Happy that the situation appeared to have been resolved, Hettie plundered the shopper with Tilly, pleased to find the steak and kidney pies which needed to be eaten. They passed one to Poppa, and Tilly placed another in front of Bruiser's nose in case he woke up hungry in the night.

Tuesday morning dawned hot and muggy. Clouds had rolled in from the sea, obscuring the sun for the first time in weeks, and Hettie woke with one of her heads. She rubbed her eyes with her paws and stretched, noticing that Tilly, who had woken even earlier, was missing from her

131

seat. The rest of the bus slept on as she made her way out into the not-so-fresh air, where she found Tilly sitting with Marley by her truck, enjoying a milky cup of tea.

'You looks like you need a mug of me best Darjeelin', Miss Hettie. Come an' sit a while. I'll put de kettle back on.'

Hettie was pleased to be off the bus and away from the rest of the travellers. The night had been strange, and a cacophony of snoring cats, punctuated by Patty Sniff talking in her sleep, had given her very little rest. Suddenly, she longed to be back in their little room in the comfort of her own armchair, with just Tilly for company. Marley's tea tasted good, though – like everything else she served up – and preparations for the tour party's breakfast were already underway. The cook opened the front of her truck, filled two huge frying pans with bacon and then cut four loaves of bread into slices. When the bacon was cooked, she made up piles of sandwiches.

'You two get your teeth round these,' she said, offering a bacon sandwich to Hettie and Tilly before taking the rest across to the bus. 'Come on!' she shouted. 'Me breakfast is served!' The cats didn't need telling twice and formed an orderly queue as Marley gave out the plates, making sure that Patty and Boobah were served first. Poppa and Bruiser chose to eat their breakfast with Hettie and Tilly, wanting to get away from the chaos on the bus. After the singalong party the night before, new friendships had been formed and the tidy seating plan that had been so carefully prepared had gone out of the back window. Derek's curtain was now completely drawn back, and his small, self-contained living area had become a comfortable, relaxed sitting room away from the hard bus seats. Suzi Quake and Deirdre Nightshade had installed themselves on Derek's Tibetan cushions, and – at his invitation – Patty Sniff was enjoying her bacon sandwich on Derek's bed. Kitty's dancers had spread themselves across the empty seats to sleep and, on Boobah's instructions, were now busy tidying up for the onward journey to Felix Toe.

'So what sort of gig are we expecting today?' asked Hettie, looking across at the activity on Derek's bus.

'Well, it's a bit hit-and-miss, this one,' said Poppa cautiously. 'The Palace in Felix Toe is usually a cinema, so the punters aren't used to gigs. I've had to do a deal on door takings with no guarantee, which is a bit of a sod, so we've just got to hope that cats will turn up. If they do, it should be a good gig – and the merch is going really well, so we might even make another killing.'

Hettie fidgeted uncomfortably, remembering that Alice Slap had been murdered and they were still no closer to knowing who had done it. There was no doubt in her mind that the perpetrator was on the tour, and Poppa's mention of another killing, no matter how out of context, reminded her that the murderer could easily strike again. Deirdre and Suzi were clearly at the top of the list of suspects, but the whole tour party had had the opportunity and possibly a hidden motive to kill Alice. The dead drummer deserved justice, regardless of how she may or may not have lived her life, and more work needed to be done.

After another round of teas and some mid-morning freshly fried doughnuts, Marley packed up her truck and the travellers took their places on the bus. Bruiser consulted the map and decided to take the scenic route to Felix Toe, hugging the coastline as far as possible to avoid the towns en route. The mood on board was a happy one and, after eating three of Marley's doughnuts, even Boobah was in high spirits – probably due to the pawful of fresh catnip that Marley had sprinkled into her batter. Tilly had seen her do it and had settled for a leftover samosa instead, not wanting to be sick; she loved the idea of catnip, but was old enough to know that it just didn't suit her.

The bus, in convoy with Marley's truck, finally pulled out of the Pavilion car park at West Grunting.

Bruiser took the cliff road down to the sea, where the clouds had finally parted to reveal a deep blue sky. The sea looked more Mediterranean than North Sea, as the sun shimmered on the water, and the gulls bobbed round in groups on the surface, chattering and screeching with the sheer joy of another hot, sunny day.

Poppa threw all the windows open as the temperature rose. Patty had given up with her Braille edition of *The Scratcher in the Rye* and was putting the book to more practical use as a fan. Derek and Suzi were closeted at the back of the bus, practising magic tricks, and his whole personality had changed in the space of a few hours. He hadn't stopped smiling since Belisha's departure, and Suzi was certainly making a play for him. Hettie dozed in the heat, occasionally opening one eye to look at the scenery. By the time they reached the outskirts of Felix Toe, she was bored with sea views and keen to investigate another paper bag or two from the tartan shopper. 'The cheese rolls aren't going to last in this heat,' said Tilly. 'I think we'd better have those now. The sweet items all look okay, but the iced fancies got a bit bashed up when the tyre blew out.'

Hettie didn't mind what she had, as long as she had it. Tilly passed one of the cheese rolls to Patty, happy to share as long as no one else noticed, and Patty was grateful – not just for the roll, but also for Tilly's unconditional friend-ship. She had spent much of her adult life being used by musicians who wanted to climb the shaky industry ladder or ignored by cats who couldn't deal with her disability; there was an innocence and a kindness to Tilly that were very rare in Patty's world, and she appreciated both.

The convoy made slow progress down the bustling High Street of the seaside town, and the cats of Felix Toe stared as the flower-power bus and Marley's truck pushed through the shoppers. The Palace Cinema stood at the top of the High Street, another example of faded decadence. Poppa was pleased to see that someone had taken the trou-ble to make a poster, which had been hurriedly slapped on the venue's double doors – but on closer inspection, it announced that night as bingo night. Bruiser drove to the back of the building, leaving space for Marley to park alongside, and Poppa leapt off the bus, telling everyone to stay put while he went to investigate. Hettie followed, knowing that he might need moral support. As in West Grunting, the front doors were locked and there was no one around, and Poppa shook his head in disbelief at the bingo poster.

'I suppose this *is* the venue?' queried Hettie.

'Yup, it's definitely the Palace Cinema, as was, but I can't work out why they think they're having a bingo night. I knew this gig was going to be a bit of a risk, but the cat

I fixed it up with seemed really keen to have us. Travis Bundy, his name is, and he's supposed to meet us here.'

'Sorry I'm a bit late,' came a familiar voice from behind them. Poppa and Hettie turned to see Ronnie Shortcrust offering a welcoming smile. 'I expect you thought you'd seen the last of me,' he continued, 'but Travis Bundy's been held up on his rollercoaster. He owns most of the seaside funfair as well as the Palace, and I help him out when he's busy.'

Poppa was in no mood to hear any more about Travis Bundy and his empire of Felix Toe amusements; there were far more pressing issues. He had a bus full of entertainers and a gig that had been hijacked by a bingo evening. 'Look, Flaky, this poster say it's bingo tonight, so where does that leave us?'

Flaky stared at the poster. 'I see what you mean, but at least you should have a good turnout – they love their bingo round here.'

Poppa resisted the urge to flatten Flaky on the pavement there and then, choosing instead to ignore his last remark. 'Well, what do you suggest we do? Shall we get the gear in or all go down to the sea for a paddle and a go on Travis Bundy's rollercoaster?'

'I think we're already on that,' said Hettie. 'Just the paddling to go.'

Her sarcasm went way over Flaky's head and he gleefully produced a bunch of keys from his pocket. 'I think we should get the gear in and hope for the best. No point in getting upset until there's a good reason for it, and I always like to look on the bright side.'

Stunned by his lack of understanding, Poppa and Hettie followed him round the back of the venue to the bus.

Boobah was waiting at the top of her ramp to roll into the car park, which was one of the things she now looked forward to each day. Seeing Hettie and Poppa returning with Flaky, she took that as her cue to set her wheels in motion and gathered speed as she hurtled down the ramp. It was Flaky who took most of the impact when the dancing mistress's wheelchair veered off course and crashed into the back of his legs. He recovered sufficiently to open the stage door, but was seen rubbing his injuries throughout the evening, whenever he had a minute to spare. Boobah suffered nothing more than a disappointment, since her bid for the wheelchair speed record had been temporarily scuppered.

The Palace Cinema's backstage area was a rabbit warren of dingy, distempered corridors, all painted chocolate brown with sludge-green skirting boards. Flaky negotiated them as if he lived there, and eventually brought Poppa and Hettie out onto the stage. It was dark, so Flaky pulled a giant lever in the wings to turn on the power, before selecting a number of switches to light the stage and auditorium. Hettie stared out at the rows and rows of seats, noting that the Palace was at least twice the size of West Grunting's Pavilion. 'There is a green room of sorts,' said Flaky brightly. 'Actually, it's a brown room, but it's just off the stage so not far to go for changeovers.'

Hettie and Poppa followed the direction that Flaky's paw had indicated and then wished they hadn't bothered: the brown room smelt of damp carpet and old furniture, and made Derek's bus look like a five-star hotel. There was a badly stained sink pulled half-away from the wall, two upright chairs – both with broken seats – and a stack of usherettes' ice-cream trays, abandoned when the cinema shut its doors. The room had no windows, and the combination of heat and damp made Hettie want to retch. She turned on her heel, quickly followed by Poppa, and rejoined Flaky on the stage; at least there was a little more air there, although the whole place smelt stale and unloved.

'Let's get the gear in and worry about the audience later,' said Poppa, trying to remain positive.

'We could ask Bruiser to take Cormac or Tarmac and plaster the town in our posters, starting with the front of this place,' said Hettie. 'The sooner we get that bloody bingo poster down, the better. I don't think the legs-eleven brigade is our core audience.'

'Brilliant plan!' said Poppa.

The three cats emerged into the sunlight to find Marley setting up for afternoon tea. She'd prepared several batches of scones and was baking them off. Tilly had been sent into the High Street to purchase cartons of fresh cream and pots of local jam to go with them, and had taken Enya to help carry the shopping. The rest of the company was milling around in the car park, waiting to be invited in. Poppa opened the side of the bus and pulled out a roll of posters, and he and Hettie scribbled 'Tonight!' across them in big letters. Bruiser was happy to fly-post them and Derek stepped forward to help, keen for a little time away from Suzi.

Tilly returned with the glad tidings that everyone in the supermarket was looking forward to the bingo evening. She'd been held up for some time at the checkout while three elderly cats discussed the possibility of getting lucky with the cat on the till, who was also hoping that her numbers would come up. Poppa looked at the gear that was still to be unloaded from the bus, trying to decide whether it was worth the effort of setting up. Hettie was right: a bingo crowd wasn't going to appreciate Patty's style of music, although Magical Mystery Paws and the Irish dancers might be right up their street. There was no doubt that they could put on a show, but it might need rejigging. With the help of Cormac, Tarmac, Flaky and the sack barrow, the gear was hauled through the corridors and onto the stage. It was going to be a night to remember, but for all the wrong reasons.

Chapter Eighteen

'You mean you don't want me to go on at all?' said Patty, biting into one of Marley's scones.

Poppa had tried to break the news to the punk star gently, but there was no easy way of telling her that she wasn't required. 'The thing is, I don't want to put you in front of a hostile audience. Last night they'd all come to see you; tonight, if anyone comes at all, they're expecting bingo. We've stuck some posters out but it's all a bit late. I've set the gear up just in case, and you can do a soundcheck if you like, but I want you to be prepared to give this one a miss.'

Poppa's conversation was rudely interrupted by a cat in a very loud checked suit, who tapped him on the shoulder with a fat paw. 'I gather you're in charge of the spectacle this evening, according to Mr Shortcrust?'

Poppa nodded and the portly cat continued. 'I note that my bingo poster has been removed from the front doors and replaced with a lurid piece of propaganda to dissuade my regular Tuesday audience from attending. I trust that Travis Bundy knows nothing of this circus that you're planning to put on?'

'Actually, he booked us to play here, so I think there's been a bit of a mix-up, Mr… er…?'

'Chesney Lacklustre is my name, and bingo is my game.'

Poppa tried desperately not to laugh, but Patty attempted no such self-control. She threw her head back and snorted with merriment, spraying Chesney Lacklustre with fresh cream, as she was eating her scone at the time.

'Sorry about that,' said Poppa, trying to remain polite and leading the checked suit away from the tour party. 'The fact is, we've been double-booked, and it seems to me that we all need to make the best of it. We could share the evening, with you going on first?'

Chesney Lacklustre was not easily placated and made that clear. 'The fact is, you can load all these ridiculous misfits onto that ridiculous bus and go back to where you came from. I'm not sharing anything.'

Bruiser had been listening in on Poppa's conversation and decided to add a little muscle, as only he could. 'Look 'ere, no need ta be rude. You don't want that nice checked suit messin' up, do yer, after I've rolled yer across the car park. Nothin' violent, mind – just a bit of fun. Or maybe you'd like ta try one of these nice cream scones and a cuppa tea before you set your stuff up?'

'Don't you try threatening me with cream cakes! I've met your sort before.'

'Then you'll know I ain't jokin',' said Bruiser, moving a little closer to the suit.

Realising that he was beaten, Chesney accepted the scone that Bruiser had proffered and disappeared through the stage door to set up his bingo machine. 'Nice one,' said Poppa gratefully, and Bruiser offered him an almost toothless grin. He had been a fine fighter in his time, needing to protect his territories, and the likes of Chesney Lacklustre were very small fry indeed.

Poppa called the company together and laid out his plan for the evening. The bingo would go ahead for the first hour, finishing in time for a brief interval. Kitty's dancers would then give a display, followed by a short performance from Magical Mystery Paws, assisted by Suzi Quake. If any punk fans did happen to turn up, there would then be the option for a quick set from Patty. They would split whatever door money there was with Chesney Lacklustre, and just make the best of a bad job.

Derek was a little taken aback at the thought of a proper performance, but he felt more confident after Belisha's departure, and Suzi had added a youthful sparkle to the act. She was also very good at card tricks, learnt from hours spent travelling to gigs, and that was an art which Derek had never quite mastered.

Marley announced that she would be preparing a late supper of her famous jerk chicken after the evening performance, which suited everyone, as they were still full from her cream tea. Patty was getting used to the idea of having an evening off, and decided to settle herself down on Derek's bed to finish reading *The Scratcher in the Rye* and do a bit of knitting. Deirdre had taken the news badly and was sulking in her seat on the bus, mainly because Suzi seemed to be carving a new career out for herself as Magical Mystery Paw's assistant. A single Cheese Triangle didn't quite have the same ring about it.

At precisely seven o'clock, a horde of Felix Toe's elderly cats alighted from the double-decker bus which stopped outside the Palace. With walking frames, sticks and at least two fold-up wheelchairs, they advanced on the cinema, forcing their way through the double doors and crushing Flaky against the wall in the foyer. He pushed his way to the box office to take the money, and issue tickets and bingo cards as fast as he could. There was an urgency about the elderly patrons, who all wanted to get a good seat and sharpen their pencils ready for eyes down at seven-thirty.

Poppa watched from the main entrance, desperately trying to spot a cat who was under pension age. It was clear that he'd made the right decision in giving Patty and her band the night off, but he was now concerned about the possibility of a riot breaking out when the audience discovered that their bingo night had been shortened to accommodate a magic act and a troupe of Irish dancers. Clearly, the posters had had little effect; they had been put up too late to turn the tide of elderly gamblers that was now streaming into the venue.

Tilly checked that there was nothing Patty needed, before joining Hettie, who had bagged a couple of house seats on the back row. As a treat, she had bought two bingo cards on the principle that if you can't beat them, join them. Much to the annoyance of the cats in the row in front, she'd also brought two bags of crisps from the tartan shopper, which she and Tilly enjoyed as noisily as they could while Chesney Lacklustre was doing his warm-up. Licking the salt off their paws, they watched the giant bingo machine rise up out of the stage, giggling as the spotlight fell on the caller. There would have been a standing ovation, such was his popularity, but most of the audience had difficulty in standing at all. Nevertheless, Lacklustre strutted and preened across the stage, enjoying the power of the followspot. Yet again, Flaky was doing a grand job from the lighting tower, where Bruiser had also decided to spend the evening.

'This is more like one of those bloody evangelical prayer meetings than a bingo session,' said Hettie. 'Just look at them, worshipping the ground he walks on. He'll be asking the cats in wheelchairs to stand up and walk next.'

'Maybe we should get Boobah and Patty a seat at the front, if he's handing out miracles,' suggested Tilly, before the cat in front swivelled round and hissed at her.

'And now the moment you've all been waiting for!' boomed Chesney Lacklustre. 'Eyes down for a full house!'

The audience fell silent as the bingo machine came to life – a giant glass aquarium filled with coloured balls dancing on a jet of hot air. The first ball fell into the chute and Chesney retrieved it. 'On the blue, naughty…?'

'Forty!' the audience shouted back at him.

Tilly and Hettie checked their numbers without success, as the caller pulled another ball from the machine. 'Made in heaven?'

'Sixty-seven!' came the response.

'Ooh! I've got that one!' said Tilly, marking her card.

'Jump and jive?'

'Thirty-five!'

'And that one!' said Tilly.

'Stuck in a tree,' continued Chesney.

'Fifty-three!' the audience screamed back at him.

'I don't believe it! I've got that one as well!' squealed Tilly.

'Duck and dive!'

'Twenty-five!'

Hettie moved forward in her seat to check Tilly's card. She only needed two more numbers to complete a line, but twenty-five wasn't there.

'Tickle me!'

'Sixty-three!'

'I've got it!' said Tilly, desperately trying to contain herself. 'Just one more to go!'

Hettie was beginning to realise just how intoxicating bingo could be. She was on the edge of her seat, willing the machine to spit out sixty-one, the final number on Tilly's line.

'Cup of tea?' Chesney barked.

'Number three!' came the reply.

'House!' shouted a cat in the front row.

A collective sigh of disappointment filled the auditorium. Tilly went one better and was heard to exclaim, 'Bugger!' as her hopes were dashed.

Chesney Lacklustre stopped the machine and made his way down the steps at the side of the stage to check the winning numbers while the audience talked amongst themselves. Hettie craned her neck to see what was happening, noting that Chesney was shaking his head. Seconds later he was back up on stage with an announcement. 'I'm afraid we've had an incorrect call,' he said. 'Please resume the game.' The bingo machine started again and another ball tumbled out into Chesney's fat paw. Tilly and Hettie held their breath for a second time as he shouted, 'Baker's bun!'

Having no idea what baker's bun corresponded with, they waited for the crowd to respond loud and clear: 'Sixty-one!'

Tilly leapt up as Hettie shouted house for her. Again, a mean-spirited sigh of disappointment filled the venue, as Tilly forgot her arthritis and bounded to the front, where Chesney was waiting to check her numbers. If he'd known that she was part of Poppa's tour, the outcome would have been very different, but – assuming she was a bona fide member of his audience – he returned to the stage, waving her card and announcing that the first game had been won with a prize of twenty pounds. Taking the money out of his checked jacket pocket, he invited Tilly up onto the stage and counted the notes into her paw. Hettie cheered from the back row, as the rest of the audience offered a somewhat muted response of polite clapping.

Tilly returned triumphantly to much hissing from the cats seated around her; bingo was clearly a game peppered with a few winners and some very bad losers. 'Come on,' said Hettie. 'Let's get out of here before you're lynched. I think we've overstayed our welcome.'

Tilly was pleased to leave the auditorium. Her win had made her hot and bothered, and it was much more pleasant by Marley's truck, where the rest of the tour party chatted happily while Derek and Suzi tried out new card tricks on them. Deirdre watched from the bus, seething at how easily her bandmate had ingratiated herself into Derek's life. She'd already blotted her copybook with Patty, and now Suzi was enjoying pastures new. Hot tears filled her eyes, and for the first time she cried for the death of Alice.

Chesney Lacklustre overran his allotted time by ten minutes, and if it hadn't been for Bruiser's sudden appearance in the wings, he might have gone on all night. He quickly brought the game they were playing to a conclusion and announced the interval. As the bingo machine sank back into the bowels of the stage, Flaky sprang out to announce a very special treat. 'We are delighted to tell you that the world-famous Magical Mystery Paws and Kitty O'Shea's Irish dance troupe are here this evening to entertain you.'

The audience members were already leaving their seats, having got what they'd come for, and only a few cats stayed put. Flaky nodded to Enya, who was in place at her keyboard, and she instantly started up the first jig. Poppa pushed the faders on the mixing desk up as loud as they would go and Kitty led out her dancers. The audience stopped in their tracks, bemused at first, but some wandered back to their seats and others stood in the gangway, undecided. Several cats at the front started clapping along, and a grey old cat with most of his whiskers missing pulled a pair of spoons out of his pocket and began to add some percussion. Bit by bit, most of the cats resumed their seats, agreeing that the dancers were worth staying for; by the time the last dance came, they'd quite forgotten they'd paid for a bingo evening.

As the last of Kitty's troupe bobbed off the stage, the audience was keen to see what would happen next. Poppa had instructed Derek to waste no time in coming on, and as Flaky was now back in the lighting box, Suzi stepped out to make the announcement, looking every bit the magician's assistant in a hurriedly put-together dress made of tin foil that sparkled under the lights. 'Please welcome to the stage the one and only Magical Mystery Paws!' she shouted into the microphone, and the audience responded with an enthusiastic round of applause.

Hettie, Tilly, Boobah and the dancers watched from the wings as Suzi and Derek worked the crowd – involving them in tricks, inviting them up on stage, pulling coins from behind their ears and eventually incorporating Derek's magic box. The knife trick brought gasps from the audience, as Derek plunged the blades into the box – apparently using Suzi as a pincushion – and all were relieved when she appeared none the worse for her experience. The final trick went down a storm. Suzi climbed back into the box as Derek finally managed to speak into the microphone, announcing that he was going to make his assistant disappear. Amid cries of dissent, he shut the door of the box and circled it, occasionally tapping the sides with his magic wand. In a flash of bingo-inspired genius, he invited the audience to say the magic word he'd chosen. 'Bibble bobble!' he shouted.

'Bibble bobble!' they cried back.

'Bibble *bobble*?' Hettie mumbled from the wings. 'What sort of magic word is that?'

'Shush,' said Tilly, sucked in by Derek's performance.

The silence in the auditorium was almost deafening, as Derek slowly opened the front of the magic box to reveal nothing. Suzi had indeed disappeared, and the cats in the audience showed their appreciation by gasping and throwing their paws up in the air. Derek moved to the front of the stage. 'Shall I see if I can bring her back?'

There was a resounding 'yes', so he repeated his circling of the box, taking care to go the other way round, as Suzi had suggested, for dramatic effect. Again, he invited the crowd to shout his magic word. 'Bibble bobble!' they chorused, and Suzi stepped from the box to the delight of everyone except Deirdre, who stood scowling at the back of the hall.

The audience at the Palace went home happy, and Poppa was so relieved to have averted a disaster that he invited Chesney to join the tour party for supper. He was delighted to accept and even helped with the packing up on stage. All were keen to get to Marley's jerk chicken, so the clearing of the stage was done in record time and the gear was neatly stacked by the stage door, ready for Poppa and Bruiser to pack it back into the bus.

Tilly had had a lovely evening and was keen to put her bingo winnings in a safe place before going to eat. The car park was dark after the lights of the Palace and it took her a moment to adjust her eyes. There were no lights on in Marley's truck, as she'd locked it up to see the show, but curiously the bus was in darkness, too. Tilly felt a little nervous as she approached it, but suddenly realised that Patty wouldn't need any lights on. Laughing at her own stupidity, she moved towards the door and fell headlong over something. To her horror, she realised that it was Patty, so she pulled herself up and shouted for help. Patty was very still and Tilly shook her, but she remained unresponsive. Leaving the star where she lay, Tilly ran the length of the car park back to the stage door, where Hettie and Poppa were just coming out. She was out of breath, but Hettie could see from the state she was in that something terrible had happened. 'What have you done to yourself?' she cried. 'You're covered in blood!'

Still gasping for breath, Tilly looked down at her paws and then to the front of her T-shirt. 'It's not my blood,' she explained. 'It's Patty's. I think she's dead over there by the bus.'

Poppa and Hettie flew in the direction that Tilly's bloody paw had indicated. Vaulting over Patty's body, Poppa leapt onto the bus to put the emergency lights on and suddenly the gruesome scene became clear. The punk star lay face down at the bottom of the bus's steps and the blood appeared to be coming from her head. Hettie crouched down, lifting Patty's paw to see if there was any sign of life; it was cold and clammy, and Hettie wasn't entirely sure but she thought there was a very faint pulse.

Poppa fetched a blanket from Derek's bed, and he and Hettie gently rolled Patty onto it while Tilly looked on. There was a large cut on the side of her head and it was still oozing blood. 'That's a good sign,' said Hettie. 'Cats don't bleed if they're dead. Her heart must still be beating.'

As if in response to Hettie's comment, the punk star began to come round. 'What's happening? Did I miss the gig? Where am I?' she said weakly.

Relieved to see that her new friend was still alive, Tilly bent low over her to offer reassurance, while Hettie returned to the stage door in search of a first-aid box. The dancers were all congregating in the corridor, and Hettie sent them off in different directions to find anything resembling a bandage. It was Marley who came to the rescue. She was chatting with Derek on stage when the news reached her and she strode across the car park to help. 'Me got plenty medical stuff in me truck from me nursin' days back in Jamaica. Take de keys and get me dat old brown box under me driver's seat – quick!' she urged, pushing her truck keys at Poppa. He returned minutes later and Marley set to work, cleaning Patty's wound and dressing it. The singer was very weak and began to shiver. 'She in shock and she lost a lot of de blood. Me tinks we should make her more comfortable in de bus. At least de bleedin' stopped.'

On Marley's instructions, Hettie and Poppa gently lifted Patty up, using the blanket as a stretcher. They carried her onto the bus and settled her down on Derek's bed. By now the tour party had gathered outside the vehicle, staring down at the pool of blood which Patty had left behind. There were mixed reactions: Suzi was hysterical and crying all over Derek's shoulder; Boobah sat in her wheelchair, shaking her head from side to side and muttering in Russian; and Enya and Aisling were being sick, as neither of them could cope with the sight of blood.

Tilly went back into the venue to clean herself up in the brown room's apology for a sink. She was surprised to find Deirdre sitting with her head in her paws on one of the broken chairs. 'She's dead, isn't she?' she said, as Tilly came through the door. 'I knew as soon as I looked at her – all that blood.'

'No,' said Tilly. 'She's not dead. Marley's looking after her, but I think we got to her in time. She's come round and everything. I think she must have slipped on the bus's steps and banged her head.'

'So you think it was an accident?'

Tilly looked into Deirdre's face, finding it impossible to read. 'Of course it was an accident. What else could it have been?'

Deirdre smiled and left the room, and a chill made its way down Tilly's spine.

Chapter Nineteen

Supper was a quiet affair. No one had much of an appetite, and it was unanimously decided that the jerk chicken could wait until the next day. Having nibbled their way through leftover scones and samosas, the tour party climbed aboard the bus and settled down quietly to rest. Marley stayed at Patty's bedside, ably assisted by Tilly throughout the night. Derek was more than happy to relinquish his personal space in the hope that Patty would make a full recovery.

Because of the disastrous end to what had turned out to be a triumphant evening, Flaky had gone home with Poppa's share of the takings. He returned to the Palace car park the next morning, hoping to catch the bus before the tour rolled on, and found Hettie and Poppa deep in conversation outside Marley's truck; sleep had been hard to find, and they had both risen early. 'How's the patient?' Flaky asked, pulling up a chair in an uninvited sort of way.

'Very confused, but at least she survived the night,' said Hettie, hugging her mug of tea. 'Marley and Tilly have been sitting with her. They've been amazing.'

'So what are you going to do without your star turn?'

'To be honest, we've no idea at present,' Poppa admitted. 'We're supposed to be playing Wobbleswick village hall tonight to a sell-out audience. They're all expecting Patty to do her stuff and she's lying half-conscious in the back of Derek's bus.'

'I wouldn't have had that lot down as a punk crowd,' said Flaky. 'They usually like their folk rock in that neck of the woods. They all live in those Arse and Craft houses, built by the Pre-Ruffleites. Wobbleswick's full of them.'

Hettie didn't even have the strength to laugh at Flaky's take on the history of art, but his comments on the village's musical taste did make her wonder why Poppa had included Wobbleswick on the tour. Poppa had no interest in art as such, but an idea was beginning to form in the back of his mind. Seeing that Hettie and Poppa were too distracted by the night's events to keep up much of a conversation, Flaky dug his paw into his pocket and pulled out a bundle of notes. 'I almost forgot why I'm here – last night's takings, split down the middle between you and Chesney.'

Poppa took the money, impressed by Flaky's honesty: it was rare to meet a venue custodian who went out of his way to settle up and, with Patty at death's door, he'd quite forgotten that they hadn't been paid. Flaky stood up to go but then turned back. 'I'll miss you all tonight. I was beginning to feel part of the tour, what with helping out and all that.'

'Why don't you come with us as a roadie?' Poppa suggested. 'We can always use another pair of paws, and we've got space on the bus.'

Flaky's face lit up as if he'd had a win on a scratch card. 'I'd love to, but I'll have to pick up some gear. How long have I got?'

'I shouldn't think we'll be going anywhere for at least an hour, but we do need to get to Wobbleswick before lunch. I've got to meet the caretaker of the hall at twelve – Miss Leek, her name is.'

'Oh, yes, I know her. Old Agnes Leek had the keys to that hall almost before it was built. A pillar of the community, though – nothing gets past her. I'll be back in forty minutes. Don't go without me.' Flaky waved to Bruiser, who was just coming down the steps of the bus, and then clambered onto an old motorbike and roared off down the High Street, delighted to have got himself a place on the Summer of Fluff Tour.

''E's in a bit of a hurry,' said Bruiser, pulling a chair into the sun. 'Nice cat – no side to 'im. We've 'ad some good chats about bikes an' that. 'E's bin teachin' me how to run stage lights. I'll miss 'im.'

'You don't have to – Poppa's just taken him on for the rest of the tour,' Hettie said.

'We're goin' on with it, then?' Bruiser looked more than a little surprised. 'I thought we'd be knockin' it on the 'ead, what with Patty and that knock on 'er 'ead. We're runnin' out of performers.'

'I admit that would be the sensible thing to do,' said Poppa, 'but there's a lot of talent on the tour that we haven't even tapped into yet.'

'So what are you suggesting?' asked Hettie. 'Moya and Aisling doing some juggling? Or maybe Boobah could do a high-wire act in her wheelchair? The possibilities are endless.'

Poppa ignored Hettie's sarcasm and cut straight to the point. 'If the good cats of Wobbleswick like folk rock, then why don't we give them folk rock? We've got a drummer, a bass player, a lead guitarist, a keyboard player and one of the finest folk rock singers ever to grace a stage.'

Hettie looked from Poppa to Bruiser: both were sporting wide grins. 'You don't mean... No, you can't mean me!' she exclaimed, spilling the rest of her tea down her T-shirt. 'I haven't done a gig for ages, and what about the band? They don't know my stuff. No, I just couldn't, and that's all there is to it.'

Poppa stood up, putting his sad face on especially for Hettie's benefit. 'Oh, well,' he said despondently. 'It was worth a try, but if you don't want to save the tour then there's nothing I can do about it. I'll go and tell the others we're heading home. We'll just have to cut our losses and run.'

Poppa walked away slowly, giving Hettie enough time to reconsider. His foot was on the first step of the bus before she relented. 'All right, you win!' she shouted after him. 'But I'll need a guitar and all afternoon to rehearse with the band, and I'm only doing a short set.' Poppa ran back to Hettie and lifted her off her chair, whirling her round in a celebratory dance, and Bruiser clapped his paws. Tilly stumbled out of the bus, rubbing her eyes after her night's vigil and wondering what her three friends had found to be so pleased about. Poppa broke the news and Tilly was delighted; she'd missed out on Hettie's music days, but now she had a chance to see her friend in a completely different light.

Tilly had had very little time to talk to Hettie after discovering Patty in the car park, but now she could see that her friend had other worries to contend with, like revamping her music career from a standing start. Her brief conversation with Deirdre in the brown room was troubling her and she feared for Patty, who had had such a narrow escape; if it wasn't an accident, had Alice's killer struck again? Tilly knew she would have to give Hettie the space she needed to sort her band out, but in the meantime she resolved to keep a very close eye on Patty.

Marley was next off the bus, keen to get breakfast under way while her patient was sleeping. When a mountain of pancakes had been cooked and devoured, Poppa called everyone together. His new strategy was well received by Suzi, Cormac and Enya, who were all very excited at the prospect of backing Hettie. Enya admitted to having several of Hettie's albums in her collection, Cormac had once had a small folk band of his own and Suzi was keen to develop her skills in as many directions as possible. Derek proffered his acoustic guitar for Hettie to play, and she accepted gratefully. Only Deirdre maintained the same sulky face that she'd worn for days, shrugging her shoulders as if she couldn't care less.

Flaky arrived with his tour duffel bag and settled himself into the seat behind Bruiser so that they could talk on the way to Wobbleswick. He abandoned his motorbike in the car park, hoping to pick it up on the way back from his adventure. Satisfied that Patty was off the danger list, Marley left Tilly to look after her while she packed her truck up ready for the journey. Hettie decided to sit with her new band and talk through some of the songs for the show, but still Deirdre showed very little interest, pretending to fall asleep so that she didn't have to respond to anything. Patty dozed peacefully, waking now and again to wonder where she was.

* * *

The tour rolled on to the little village of Wobbleswick, which nestled on the coast. The main street was peppered with some oddly designed houses, and Flaky – who'd been there on a number of occasions – turned tour guide, giving a running commentary as the bus progressed. 'Left and right you can see the Arse and Craft houses – they're the ones with silly round windows and balconies going nowhere. They were designed by some Scottish cat called Redgie Mackintosh. The village is famous for its annual crabbing competition. The idea is that the cat who catches the biggest crab within half an hour takes it home for his tea. The rest of the crabs are sold off to pay for the upkeep of the village hall. Probably the most interesting fact about Wobbleswick is the phantom coach driven by the murderer Tobias Gulp, who was hanged in these parts back in the eighteenth century. Strange, really, as the coach is pulled by a set of headless horses. I don't quite see how they know where they're going, but that's the story. And just here on the right is our destination: Wobbleswick village hall.' Flaky's little points of history had kept everyone entertained, and by the time the bus drew into the car park, swiftly followed by Marley's truck, the whole tour party had cheered up and was ready to do battle on day three of their epic journey.

Agnes Leek was waiting and had been for some time, as she liked to be an hour ahead of herself in all things. Her timekeeping played havoc with her meals, embarrassed her kittens – who used to be dropped off at the village school an hour before it opened – and convinced everyone around her that they were late. Now she was older and her kittens were long gone, she took it upon herself to run the village to a strict hour-ahead timetable. Thanks to extortionate house prices which very few could afford, Wobbleswick boasted some rather famous residents: TV stars, film-makers, artists and authors lived behind the polished door knockers, busy pursuing their careers and only coming out of their expensive cocoons when they felt like it. Collectively, they had chosen to ignore Agnes's regime, but were perfectly happy for her to deal with incoming strangers – a paws-off approach which gave Agnes the power she craved whilst preserving the invisibility that the artisan and celebrity cats enjoyed. Tonight, the great and the good would all be at the village hall, but surprisingly Agnes herself had forgotten to buy a ticket in advance and faced an evening at home with her miniature cacti.

Poppa was first off the bus, keen to explain to their host that there'd been a slight amendment to the programme. Miss Leek viewed him with suspicion at first, mainly because of the highly decorated bus he'd alighted from, but formalities were exchanged and Agnes relaxed. Poppa noticed that there was a definite lilt to her voice, which he found rather attractive; to curry favour, he complimented her on her accent and she was proud to announce that her family had come from a farm in the Welsh hills. She pulled the village hall keys from her apron pocket – she found an apron reassuring, even when she went out, as life could be messy – and Poppa waited at the entrance to be invited in. Agnes moved around the hall, switching the lights on while the sun beamed in through the high windows, casting patterns on the parquet floor. 'I'm puttin' these on now, see, in case you can't find them later,' she said, beckoning Poppa into the hall. 'Over there is the kitchen – just tea an' coffee, mind. We don't hold with cookin', as we burnt the last village hall down, see. When I say "we", I mean the Wobbleswick Film Society. They 'ad one of those themed evenin' dos, an' they were fryin' green tomatoes for some reason. Took their eye off for a minute, they did, an' the whole place went up like matchwood.'

Poppa tutted in the right places, waiting for an opportunity to discuss the change of plan for the evening. Eventually it came, and he ploughed in with both paws. 'We've had a bit of a disaster with our star vocalist, Miss Patty Sniff…'

'Sniff, you say?' interrupted Agnes. 'Not the Sniffs of Pontimog, is it? Well, I never – all singers, they were. Raised in the valleys you couldn't help it, see.'

Poppa waited again for Agnes to take a breath and dived into the somewhat one-sided conversation. 'I'm not sure where the family came from, but Patty had an accident last night in Felix Toe and is still recovering. She won't be able to sing tonight.'

'Accident, you say? Well, that comes as no surprise to me – Felix Toe's a strange place at the best of times.

Funfairs an' slots – just encouragin' the gambling, see. Cold beach, too, not like we got here. Dunes make all the difference, see. You can get down out of the wind.'

Poppa desperately tried to look interested, but he was aware of how little time Hettie had to lick her band into shape. He'd promised her a long rehearsal, and Agnes Leek – nice as she seemed – wasn't helping. Realising that the caretaker had no real interest in the acts he was putting on, he tried a different tack. 'Would it be okay if we brought the equipment in now? We're keen to get it set up and have a practice.'

'A practice, you say? Not too loud, mind. We're not used to noise round here. Anyway, you've kept me talkin' long enough. I might pop back later to see how you're gettin' on, like, but I'm due at the tea shop in an hour to help with the lunches.' Poppa was relieved to be rid of his new friend. He watched as she crossed the village green and disappeared into a tea shop, where she was obviously going to be an hour early.

The call to arms was swift and involved everyone except Patty and Boobah. In record time, the gear was brought in, and Hettie and Poppa wired the stage while Flaky and Bruiser put the heavier equipment in place. The stage was small and Poppa decided to put the dancers on the floor in front of it, much to Boobah's annoyance. He was getting used to her protestations by now and pointed out discreetly that everyone had to make sacrifices, including her; she could have replied that she'd already lent him Enya and Cormac, but he walked away before she had the chance.

Within an hour, the stage was set for Hettie's band to rehearse. Marley had revived the jerk chicken from the night before and, after a relaxed lunch in the sun, the tour party split up. Hettie, Suzi, Deirdre, Cormac and Enya headed for the stage, while Poppa stationed himself at the mixing desk, and the dancers struck out for the sand dunes and the sea, with Derek pushing Boobah. Hettie had made it clear to Poppa that she didn't want an audience for her rehearsals, and he'd given all those not involved some time off.

Tilly took a dish of Marley's chicken to Patty, who made a good fist of it. She looked brighter, but the confusion persisted, and Tilly had to keep reassuring her that she was safe and out of danger. She was hoping for a lucid moment when Patty could recall the exact circumstances of her fall, but rest was the priority at the moment. Deciding to give Hettie's rehearsals a miss in favour of the real show later, Tilly settled herself on a cushion at the bottom of Patty's bed to read Nicolette Upstart's novel, *Nine Lives*. Nicolette had been all over TV and radio with her new book, much to the delight of Tilly, who had spent time with the author at the town's literary festival and felt that she knew her. The book opened with a nasty murder in a graveyard and a cat who had been buried alive; Tilly lapped it up until things turned even nastier and she decided to have a sleep instead. She was exhausted from the night before and Patty looked peaceful, so she dozed on her cushion, ready to spring up if she was needed.

Back in the village hall, Hettie took Derek's guitar out of its case and checked the tuning. It had a nice sound, but she felt it would benefit from a change of strings. There was no time to do it now, but she would ask Poppa to take care of it for her later – after all, he'd got her into this mess in the first place. She lifted the flip-up compartment in the case, which revealed several plectrums and a spare set of strings. To her horror, she noticed that the D string was missing. The strings were bronze wound and medium gauge, just like the one that had been used to strangle Alice Slap.

'You ready to go for it?' asked Poppa, making her jump. 'I'll do the restringing later for you, if you like.'

'That would be good,' said Hettie, 'but we don't seem to have a full set. The D string is missing.'

'Blimey!' said Poppa. 'That's a turn-up for the book.'

Deirdre and Suzi had wandered over and were keen to start. 'Is there a problem with Derek's guitar?' Deirdre asked.

'Not exactly,' Hettie replied casually. 'We're short of a spare D string, but I can manage for now.' She put the guitar round her neck and got up on the stage. Suzi and Deirdre followed, and Hettie suggested a set of jigs and reels as a warm-up to allow Poppa to balance the instruments. Enya chose a couple of favourites that Boobah never let her play, and one by one – when the tune was established – the band joined in, with Hettie pounding out the rhythms on Derek's guitar. Poppa was impressed and so was Bruiser, who'd got bored with the sand dunes and Flaky's travelogue and crept in at the back of the hall. He was soon joined by Marley, who'd left a pot of beef chilli bubbling on the stove in her truck.

Poppa had quite forgotten what a hard taskmaster Hettie was when it came to her music. After the jigs, she gave the band a little talk about how important the words were in a folk song: it was a story, with a beginning, a middle and an end. Enya and Cormac nodded in agreement, Suzi listened carefully, and Deirdre fiddled with her guitar, punctuating the masterclass with the odd screaming chord.

Although Hettie's music had crossed the spectrum of genres, she had chosen to perform some of her darker, more violent ballads; they were in keeping with Patty's style, and the band seemed very receptive to her murder stories and anti-war songs. The chords and words came back to her as if they'd never been gone, but it was her voice she was most concerned about. Age changed things: high notes disappeared and low notes became richer, and she discarded one or two songs after the first run-through. Within a couple of hours, she'd put together a good set of blood-and-thunder songs, as she liked to call them. Her scratch band had risen to the plate, too, and Poppa was mentally planning a Hettie Bagshot tour, although it wasn't the time to mention it.

The dancers gradually drifted back from the sand dunes, keen to rehearse a few steps before the audience arrived. Poppa had sent Bruiser and Flaky out with updated posters, making it clear that Hettie Bagshot would be giving a rare performance due to Patty's accident. Having got Suzi back from playing in Hettie's band, Derek set up his magic box at the back of the hall and the two cats practised some tricks, adding a few new items to their performance.

Deirdre had enjoyed her rehearsals with Hettie, but tried hard not to show it. Seeing that Suzi's allegiance had shifted once again to Magical Mystery Paws, she put her guitar back into its case and headed for the bus to sulk in peace. 'How's Patty?' she called, climbing aboard and waking Tilly with a start.

Patty answered for herself. 'Oh, hi – is that you, Deirdre?' she said. 'Feeling a bit weird, actually. Getting flashing lights and really surreal dreams. Not sure if I'm awake or asleep.'

'You've got concussion,' Tilly added, as Deirdre came closer to the bed. 'You had a very nasty bang on the head when you fell down those steps.'

'Yeah, that's what happened – an accident,' said Deirdre. 'Good job Tilly here found you when she did or you'd be a goner by now.'

Patty tried to sit up, but the pain in her head was too much. Deirdre slouched back to her seat, hoping to get some sleep before the gig, and Tilly straightened the pillows. She was hungry, and longed to see how Hettie was getting on, but there was no way she was leaving Patty alone with Deirdre Nightshade. Then she remembered her tartan shopper and returned to her seat to see if there was anything left worth eating. Several paper bags remained, and she chose some bright-pink iced fancies to nibble on; they were a little tour-weary, but still tasted good. She took the bag back to her cushion and settled down with her book as Patty went back to sleep.

When Hettie returned to the bus, she was obviously pleased with how rehearsals had gone and Tilly decided that it was time to discuss the case. There were still a couple of hours to go before show time and they had both missed out on a trip to the sand dunes, so she suggested that a walk by the sea would be a good place to talk. Marley was enlisted to sit with Patty, and the two friends struck out across the sands.

The Wobbleswick dunes were peppered with black beach shacks – unattractive to look at, but offering a cheap and cheerful holiday in a place where even bed and breakfasts were too expensive for the average cat. The shacks were self-contained, offering a place to sleep, a small kitchen and a veranda for sitting out. As Hettie and Tilly made their way to the sea, they both appreciated the opportunity to escape from the tour bubble. They were surrounded by families playing in the late afternoon sun, but there was still peace to be found in the vast stretch of sand and the open sky.

'Were you pleased with your rehearsals?' Tilly asked. 'The bits I heard from the bus sounded really good, but I daren't leave Patty to come and look.'

'I think we did all right under the circumstances. They make quite a nice band, actually, and Enya's really coming out of her shell. I think Cormac's taken a fancy to her now that he's discovering some of her hidden depths.'

'What about Deirdre? Is she as sulky on stage as off?'

'I think Deirdre's problem is that she wants to be the leader of a band, not just in one. It's a shame, because she's actually a really good guitarist when she can manage to keep her paw off the volume control. I doubt that The Cheese Triangles will last beyond this tour, though.'

'Why do you say that?' Tilly asked, keen to understand more about band dynamics.

'Because Suzi's having too good a time messing about with Derek and his magic act, and she isn't paying enough attention to Deirdre and her moods. They've both fallen from grace with Patty – if she recovers, I think she'll be looking for new musicians who aren't continuingly conspiring to make it on their own. It's a filthy business and I'm pleased to be out of it, so the sooner Patty recovers, the better. I don't mind helping Poppa out tonight, but we have a murder to solve and there are still several dates to go.'

The friends had almost reached the sea, and Tilly – slightly out of breath from negotiating the sand and shingle – sat down on a tussock of grass to rest. Hettie joined her and they stared out to sea, enjoying the silver ripples as the sun played on the surface. 'Well, this is all very lovely,' Hettie said, 'and as far away from Alice Slap being strangled with a guitar string as you could get. Speaking of guitar strings, Derek has a D string missing from his spares – and judging by the state of the one on the guitar, that hasn't been changed for some time.'

Tilly digested the new information, wishing she'd brought her notepad to the beach. 'I've got Derek on my list of suspects,' she said, 'but, unlike several of the others, I can't see why he'd want to kill Alice.'

'I agree: anyone could have taken the string from his guitar case at the Methodist Hall. Cats were on and off that bus all day. What about Patty? Have you had a chance to talk to her about her fall?'

'She seems to think it was an accident – or rather, Deirdre told her it was, in a round and about way. I'm not sure why Deirdre knows so much about it, unless she was there when it happened – and if she *was* there, why didn't she call for help?'

Hettie thought for a moment, considering why Deirdre Nightshade might want Patty dead and what good it would do her. Being a key suspect in Alice's murder made sense – there could have been an issue between them or a friendship gone wrong – but Patty was a different matter. 'Why would she want to kill the goose that lays the golden eggs?' she said. 'As things stand at the moment, being in Patty's band is all that Deirdre has, especially now that Suzi seems to be branching out. There must be secrets here that we haven't tapped into yet. It's generally accepted that Alice's death was an accident, and no one is treating Patty's fall as anything but the sort of scrape she gets into every day. The tour just seems to meander on with a disaster waiting around every corner, but someone is manipulating the whole thing, including us.'

'Agatha Crispy wrote a similar story where lots of cats were murdered one by one,' Tilly said helpfully.

'And how did it end?' asked Hetty, keen to get help from anywhere, even Miss Crispy.

'Well, I guessed, of course,' said Tilly, puffing her chest out. 'It was one of the cats who'd been murdered.'

Hettie shook her head in disbelief. 'So by that reasoning, Alice Slap could be at the bottom of any murders that are still to come! Try telling that to Morbid Balm. We should give her a call and ask her to check her freezer. If Alice is missing, we'll know it was she who shoved Patty down the steps – that's if anyone *did* shove Patty down the steps.'

The two cats laughed at the pictures that Hettie had put into their minds; the scenario was beginning to sound as wild as Flaky's headless horses. 'Let's go back to the beginning,' said Hettie. 'We know that Alice had been let down by someone she'd formed an attachment to. We think that may have been Deirdre, and Deirdre has already admitted that she found Alice difficult and clingy. We know that Deirdre and Suzi both had issues with Alice, who seemed closer to Patty in her allegiances. We also know that – according to Patty – Alice went out to settle a score on the night she died and that she'd been arguing with someone about getting her own back. Now, that someone must have been on the tour, as they were all together that night. Whichever way you look at it, Deirdre is firmly in the frame.'

'Unless someone tried to frame *her*,' said Tilly. 'Suzi would know all about the goings-on in Alice's and Deirdre's lives, and she might have strangled Alice with a guitar string to put the blame on Deirdre. There's certainly no love lost there.'

'But it was made to look like a perfectly understandable accident, with a bacon sandwich stuffed in her mouth,' Hettie countered.

'Maybe it was a double bluff. She made it *look* like an accident, knowing that the guitar string would be found eventually and that the claw would then point at Deirdre.'

Hettie considered Tilly's reasoning, agreeing that it was a possibility. 'Well, if that's the case, it's backfired, because everyone except the killer *does* think it was an accident. We need to find out if Patty can remember anything about her fall. Deirdre was a loose cannon last night at Felix Toe. She had the night off, and I don't remember seeing her at the venue. Suzi was only tied up with Derek for their show, so she could have nipped out and given Patty a shove, and then carried on with the performance while Patty was dying in the car park. So far, when it comes down to it, it's all about Patty and her band, and that's where we should focus our attention.'

Tilly agreed to talk to Patty about her fall, and Hettie proposed to get closer to Suzi; now they were temporary bandmates, there would be more opportunities for 'idle' conversations.

Chapter Twenty

By the time Hettie and Tilly returned from their walk, all was set for the gig. Kitty's dancers had been put through their paces by Boobah, Derek and Suzi had rehearsed a new trick with the magic box, and Enya had borrowed a T-shirt from Suzi which was more appropriate to her new role in Hettie's band. It was doubtful that her mother back in Donegal would have approved, as the back of the T-shirt proclaimed the words 'Sod Off!', but Suzi's wardrobe had worse slogans and Enya had chosen the least offensive.

Leaving Hettie to check the stage set-up, Tilly clambered back on the bus to see how Patty was. She was delighted to find her sitting up and chatting to Marley, who looked pleased with her patient's progress. 'If you okay to sit wid Miss Patty a bit, I can go and get de dinners ready. We eatin' before de concert as dey all sayin' dey hungry. Me jerk chicken went nowhere, so I servin' me chilli wid rice. I'm plannin' hot beef sandwiches for de supper later, so I need to get me ready. Me don't want to miss Hettie on stage tonight – that goin' to be a reeeel treat.'

Marley shuffled down the gangway, leaving Tilly in charge of Patty. 'You look so much better,' she said.

The punk star was pleased to hear Tilly's voice and seemed much more receptive than earlier. 'Yeah, my head's not banging so much, but I do feel a bit strange without my shades. I must have lost them when I fell.'

Tilly sprang up. 'I can help with that,' she said, moving down the bus to her seat and grabbing her bag of bits and pieces. 'I picked them up off the floor in the car park last night, but in the panic I forgot to give them back to you.'

Tilly put the singer's dark glasses into her paws and Patty wasted no time in putting them on, taking care not to disturb the bandage on her head. 'Thank you,' she said gratefully. 'You've no idea how much better that feels. They're my comfort blanket. I might not be able to see the world, but the world sees me – and I'd rather be looking cool with my shades on when it's looking.'

Tilly laughed, but had to agree that Patty looked a whole lot better with her dark glasses. With the singer almost back to her old self, she decided that a gentle probing about the fall might be in order. She took her bag back to her seat, checked that there was no one else on the bus and returned to Patty. 'Can you remember anything about your accident?' Tilly asked, getting straight to the point.

Patty tilted her head to one side, as if she were trying to listen in on a conversation. 'The thing is, since banging my head, I've had this weird film playing out in my mind, right, and it's all a bit of a muddle. Faces I don't know coming and going, voices and colours – lots of colours. I remember reading my book and getting bored with it, and wanting to get some fresh air. It was the perfume that was getting to me, I think, and it freaked me out because I was sure it was Alice's perfume.'

'The same as the one you smelt the night she died?'

'Yeah, that's right – Reeve Gosh. Anyway, I can remember feeling my way down the bus and calling out to see if anyone was there. The door must have been open because I could hear the music from the dancers, and then it was like my legs were pulled from under me. I must have missed the steps completely, and I think I banged my head twice before passing out. I could say everything went black, but that's normal for me.' Patty laughed at her own joke but Tilly wasn't amused. The fact that the singer thought she'd banged her head twice could mean that someone had attempted to finish her off before leaving the scene, and the perfume was obviously significant. 'I've been having a bit of a think while I've been lying here,' Patty continued. 'About Alice, mainly – what if someone helped her on her way?'

'You mean murdered her?' said Tilly, trying to sound surprised.

'Yeah. I know that's a bit off the planet, but there was definitely trouble that night. Someone was getting to her big time. And then I thought, what if someone was having a go at me and shoved me down the steps? Being on this bus, I've no way of telling what's going on or who's around.'

'If that *did* happen, who would want to hurt you?' Tilly asked.

'I don't think I can answer that. In fact, I'd rather not go there. Living in the dark like I do, you always have to look on the bright side or you'd just crawl away and die from fear of the unknown. I spend my life waiting for a bus to hit me. The only good thing about that sort of attitude is that you hope, when it comes, that it will be quick and painless.'

The more time Tilly spent with Patty, the more she liked her. She was tempted to tell her what had really happened to Alice, but ignorance was probably safer at this point, even if she was increasingly convinced that Patty's fall had been no accident.

'Are you going to Hettie's gig tonight?' asked Patty.

'I'm not sure. I think Marley and me are going to take it in turns to sit with you again, but I'd like to see some of it. I didn't know her when she had her band. I've heard the albums, and seen lots of posters and photos, but it's not the same as being there.'

'She was brilliant. Believe me, she blew most of the bands off those festival stages with her stuff, and she gave me a run for my money once or twice, too. If you could find me a chair to sit on, I wouldn't mind hearing her again. You, me and Marley could sit together.'

'But are you sure you're well enough? You've only just started to feel better, and you shouldn't overdo it.'

'I'll be fine, I promise. Anyway, I'll have my two body-guards with me, won't I?'

Tilly was still a little concerned for Patty, but she was also upset at the thought of missing Hettie's big gig. At least if Patty was in the village hall with the rest of the audience, no harm could come to her. Marley appeared with two plates of chilli and rice, and made her way to the back of the bus. 'Dere you are – waitress service and me want to see clean plates. Dat me special chilli. Not too hot, just nice.'

Tilly passed one of the plates to Patty, putting a fork in her paw. Patty pulled the plate up to her chin and began scooping the food into her mouth. 'This is great,' she said between mouthfuls. 'A lot better than the tour food we used to get – if we got any at all.'

Marley was pleased to see that Patty had a good appetite and offered to sit with her while Tilly went off to eat with Hettie. Tilly was glad to take her chilli off the bus, as she didn't want to offend Marley by telling her that she didn't like it; she'd just about got used to mild curries, but chilli sounded far too frightening, and she knew that Hettie would help her out by eating an extra portion. Before she left the bus, she explained to Marley that Patty wanted to go to Hettie's gig. There was much consternation from the cook, but Patty managed to assure her that she would be okay; if she felt bad, she would ask to be brought back to the bus.

Tilly skipped off with her dinner to look for Hettie and found her eating with Poppa at the mixing desk. She joined them and scooped her chilli onto their almost empty plates. 'You'll wish you hadn't done that,' said Hettie. 'What if you're hungry later?'

'I won't be. I've already had iced fancies out of my shopper and Marley's doing hot beef sandwiches for supper. The really big news is that Patty's coming to watch you play – well, not exactly *watch* you, but she's insisting on being there to hear you. She's feeling much better, and me and Marley are going to sit with her to make sure she's all right.'

Hettie was pleased to have her friends there to support her, and Poppa responded by fetching three chairs from the back of the hall to put by the mixing desk. 'There you are,' he said. 'Three seats in the royal box. Sorted.'

Tilly clapped her paws with excitement as Agnes Leek walked into the hall, sniffing the air. 'I forgot to say,' she began, 'there's no wet food allowed in here, see. You can 'ave your crisps and biscuits – they just crumb up – but wet food is not permitted on account of the parquet floor. Gets in the cracks, see, an' that stuff you're forking in is bad for parquet floors. Takes the polish right off, it does.'

Hettie did her best not to laugh but couldn't control herself and ran for the door, trying hard not to splutter Marley's chilli all over the precious parquet floor. Tilly collected the two empty plates and followed her, leaving Poppa to deal with the caretaker.

At exactly twenty-five past seven, the doors of Wobbleswick village hall opened simultaneously and a steady train of cats made their way inside. Tilly watched from the bus, where she was attempting to comb some of the dried blood from last night's emergency out of her fur. She recognised several of the cats from the television, and those she didn't know were very well-heeled; it was clearly going to be what Tilly liked to call a 'posh event', and quite different from the crowds at West Grunting and Felix Toe.

Hettie had suddenly got an attack of nerves and was pacing up and down outside the back of the hall, where she could be on her own. She had plenty of time to collect herself, as Poppa was putting Magical Mystery Paws first on the bill to give Suzi time to change while the dancers were on. After the dancers there was to be a twenty-minute interval, and then Hettie's band.

Agnes Leek had been stationed at the door to collect tickets for the last hour and was now letting everyone in. There was a measured, almost polite, rush for the best seats at the front, and the hall filled up very quickly. Bruiser and Flaky were squashed into a tiny lighting box at the back and Poppa had agreed to announce the acts from the mixing desk. Marley, Tilly and Patty crept in at the last moment to take their seats; Agnes closed the door behind them, before making her way back to her small cottage and her cacti.

Derek and Suzi's magic act went down well – it was quite a novelty for those in the audience who spent their working lives behind and in front of film and TV cameras. When they came to their grand finale with the magic box, the knife and disappearing act worked like a dream, so Suzi whispered in Derek's ear, as the audience stood to applaud, 'Come on, they love us! Let's give them an encore. Let's do the saw trick.'

Derek gasped as Suzi lay the magic box on its side and handed him the saw which she'd made a point of bringing on with her. Jumping in and lying down, Suzi pushed open the flaps so that the audience could see her head and feet. Derek froze for a moment, knowing that the trick wasn't quite there yet, but Suzi continued to encourage him, pretending to be the damsel in distress who was about to be sawn in half by the wicked magician. The crowd was delighted with the staged drama being played out in front of them and goaded Derek on to complete the diabolical deed.

Tilly sat at the mixing desk, giving a running commentary of the action to Patty, but she froze along with Derek, putting her paws in her mouth to muffle any screams as he raised the saw to cut Suzi in half. The audience fell silent as he slotted it into a groove halfway down the box and slowly began to cut it in half. Suzi winced, and the audience responded with a collective gasp. Then she cried out, as the saw continued to make its deadly progress through the wood. Finally, she fainted and her feet twitched on their own at the other end of the box. The saw had gone all the way down and Derek took his paw away to prove it. The audience murmured as Suzi lay still. Her feet had stopped twitching, and Derek began to look concerned.

Tilly gripped Patty's paw and whispered: 'I think she's dead! He's sawn her in half!'

Poppa was also looking worried and considered asking Flaky to kill the stage lights out of decency; if the trick had failed, the cats of Wobbleswick had just witnessed a cold-blooded murder. Hettie stared at the scene in horror from the side of the stage, behind the speakers, ready to offer assistance if the trick had backfired. The murmurs were replaced by a deathly silence, and Derek stood like a condemned cat waiting for the executioner. He was suddenly afraid to withdraw the saw from the box in case it had blood on it, but he knew that he'd have to if the trick was to work. He looked down at Suzi with his back to the audience and she winked at him. In an instant he became Magical Mystery Paws again and withdrew the saw with a flourish; to his and the audience's relief, it came out clean.

Suzi sat up and the crowds got to their feet to show their appreciation. They clapped and stamped as Magical Mystery Paws offered his paw to his very glamorous assistant. She stepped out of the magic box unscathed, and the two cats took a bow. 'Blimey,' said Poppa. 'That was a close one. For a minute there, I thought he'd done for her.' Tilly pulled her paws out of her mouth and resumed her commentary for Patty, and Marley – who had spent most of the trick with her apron over her head – laughed out loud with relief. Derek and Suzi left the stage, taking their magic box with them.

Kitty's dancers were gathered in the wings and the bobbing began as soon as Enya took her place at the keyboard. They revved up, ready to spread themselves out across the floor in front of the stage, and Boobah sat in her wheelchair like a football manager on a touchline, offering instructions as the troupe began a very fine display of step dancing. The audience was thrilled with the spectacle and enjoyed every minute of it, although weeks later it was decided at the village hall committee meeting that the parquet floor wouldn't benefit from any more visiting dance troupes.

The interval was called and the audience huddled round the hatch that led through to a small kitchen, where a bespectacled elderly cat was doing her best to serve tea and pink wafer biscuits. Poppa, Bruiser and Flaky pulled the band gear to the front of the stage, and Poppa double-checked that Hettie's mic was working and that her monitor system was loud enough.

Hettie had gone back to the bus to change her T-shirt and collect Derek's guitar, and had walked in on a real catfight between Suzi and Deirdre. The two cats were hissing insults at each other, while Derek cowered at the back of the bus. Deirdre was in full flow as Hettie pushed past them to her seat, narrowly missing a slap that was meant for Suzi Quake. 'You just keep pushing your luck, don't you?' spat Deirdre. 'Making a fool of me with your stupid magic act. What sort of a tour are we on here? I signed up to back Patty Sniff, and we only played one gig with her before you turned yourself into some sort of variety end-of-pier act. What sort of street cred does that give The Cheese Triangles?'

Suzi flew at Deirdre, knocking her into one of the seats and leaning over her. 'Don't talk to me about street cred! You're the one who called us The Cheese Triangles in the first place. Alice was right: you're so uncool – and you'll never be anything else.'

Deirdre sat up, pushing Suzi away from her. 'That's right – you bring Alice into this because you can't think of anything else to say. You'd better watch your back or you'll be playing in that big band in the sky before you know it!'

'Should I take that as a threat?' asked Suzi.

Hettie decided to intervene, hoping to cool things down and knowing that the interval would soon be over. 'Okay you two – there's a hall full of cats waiting to hear some music out there. Whatever's going on between you can wait until later. Let's just get this gig over, shall we?'

Suzi grabbed her bass guitar and left the bus, followed by Derek. Deirdre stood her ground as Hettie changed her T-shirt and then offered an apology. 'I'm sorry about kicking off like that. I just feel like everything's slipping away from me.'

'Why do you say that?' asked Hettie.

'Because a couple of months ago we had a great band. We were recording with Patty and life was good… The whole thing has just exploded in my face: no one talks to me anymore, the tour seems to be all about Suzi and Alice is lying in a box somewhere.'

Hettie could see that Deirdre was close to tears, and for the first time she felt sorry for her. The guitarist would never win a prize for popularity on the tour, but it was obvious that she was in a very lonely place. The big question was: did that make her a killer?

Poppa put paid to any further conversation by coming to fetch Hettie's guitar, and the three cats left the bus together. When everything was switched on and ready to go, Hettie gave Poppa the claws up and he announced the band. 'And now we have a slight change to tonight's line-up. Miss Patty Sniff is unable to perform due to a recent accident, but we can bring you a very special replacement. Please put your paws together for The Hettie Bagshot Band!'

The audience was polite but a little disappointed and gave the band a lukewarm welcome. Undaunted, Hettie thundered out the first verse of a song which she thought would be the perfect starter.

'The world to me just seems to be an empty timeless age,
Where prophecy can never be, thus spoke the Twisted Sage.
Thus spoke the Twisted Sage.
And I have played the alchemist in dungeons of the earth,
And poisoned all humanity, and laughed for all I'm worth.
And laughed for all I'm worth.
And I have risen from the dead, each morning when I wake.
And prayed that daylight was away and darkness would me take.
And darkness would me take.'

And so the song rolled on. Hettie spat out the words, aided and abetted by her band, and created an attack on the audience which wouldn't be forgotten in a hurry. Tilly sat next to Patty, mesmerised by her friend as she dominated the crowd and brought the first song to its conclusion with a screaming solo from Deirdre. The audience was eating out of Hettie's paw and her band could do no wrong, moving seamlessly through a set which featured long and dramatic murder ballads, tales of witches and devils, and a couple of blatant rock songs.

Three encores later, Hettie finally left the stage, her fur drenched with the sweat of her labours, and Poppa dearly wished that he'd got a stack of her albums to sell. Marley wasted no time in laying out a few boxes of tour T-shirts, which she'd kept in her truck from the gig at West Grunting, and the audience bought up most of her stock as they left.

Chapter Twenty-One

With the success of the Wobbleswick gig still ringing in their ears, Poppa, Bruiser and Flaky packed down the heavy gear. Suzi and Deirdre excused themselves from helping; Suzi said they'd got a few things to sort out and were going for a walk, as it was such a warm evening. Hettie was pleased to see that the gig had acted as a sticking plaster on their differences and the two musicians left the hall, chatting amiably. Patty sat happily at the back while Tilly and Hettie coiled up some wires on the stage. Derek left his magic box by the bus, ready to pack, and then joined the dancers at Marley's truck, where the cook had promised to serve supper as soon as everyone was free.

It was another hour before the tour party enjoyed their hot beef sandwiches. Agnes Leek turned up with the takings and the keys, and engaged Poppa, Hettie and Tilly in a lengthy conversation about how long it had taken to lay the parquet floor and how much polish it consumed each year. The floor was obviously her pride and joy, and Poppa didn't have the heart or the energy to be rude.

Agnes finally handed over the money and was about to lock up when she spied Patty. Poppa felt that it was only polite to introduce her, but forgot not to mention the surname 'Sniff'. Another twenty minutes passed while Patty was given chapter and verse on the Sniff family from Pontimog, but eventually Agnes ran out of steam and locked the front door, leaving Poppa, Hettie, Tilly and Patty to make their way to supper.

Bruiser and Flaky had stacked the gear by the bus, but Poppa decided to wait until after supper to pack it away in the hold. Food had become a priority, and the smell of beef drifting from the other side of the car park was irresistible. After such a successful evening, it was a jolly supper party. Derek was reunited with his guitar and offered some chorus songs which even Boobah joined in on. There was much made of Hettie's triumphant return to music, and both Enya and Cormac said that they would be happy to join her band anytime. Deirdre and Suzi were significant by their absence; Deirdre turned up later, in time for the last beef sandwich, and said that Suzi had bumped into a friend who was staying in one of the shacks on the dunes. She'd left them talking about old times and struck out for the sea, which she'd missed earlier because of rehearsals.

Patty had done well to manage the evening and the late supper party, but Tilly could see that she was flagging and suggested that they go back to the bus to get some rest. The punk star was keen to call it a night, and the two cats left to prepare for bed. The bus was dark and Tilly clambered up the steps, feeling for the emergency light switch on the dashboard. Her paw reached for it, but in an instant she was knocked head-first down the steps, as something came at her with force from inside. The creature made its escape, treading Tilly's face into the ground as it leapt to freedom, and Patty threw her paws out wildly in an effort to help. Tilly cried out, and Hettie and Poppa flew across the car park, fearing that history was repeating itself.

'Are you all right?' asked Hettie, as Tilly wriggled in pain.

'I think so, but my paws are bleeding. I stuck them out in front of me to break my fall and they've got bits of gravel in them.'

Hettie gently pulled her friend to her feet and Poppa took Patty's paw to lead her onto the bus, stopping to put the lights on. By then, the tour party had gathered round, keen to see what had happened. At first Poppa couldn't quite take in the sight before him; he stopped dead, and Patty crashed into his back. Taking a moment to come to terms with what was all too obvious, he finally spoke. 'Well, that really is a sod.'

'What is?' asked Patty. 'What's happening? How's Tilly?'

Poppa responded, realising that Patty was still in the dark. 'Tilly's fine, except for a few cuts and grazes, but the bus is totally wrecked.'

Hettie and Tilly also clambered aboard, so Poppa and Patty moved down the aisle to make room for them. Hettie stared in horror at the mess: clothes spilling out of roof racks, books and newspapers strewn across the seats, and bags and suitcases rifled through. Tilly's tartan shopper stood upside down, and Derek's bed and cushions had been slashed, and were spilling their stuffing everywhere.

'Someone's done a real number on us,' said Poppa, parking Patty in the seat closest to him. He moved swiftly to his own seat and felt underneath it for his gig bag. It wasn't there. 'I don't believe it! My bag's gone – and so has all the tour money.' He sank down onto his seat and put his head in his paws.

Keen to get Tilly's paws seen to, Hettie helped her off the bus and Marley took her over to her truck to administer first aid. Hettie stood on the bottom step and addressed the rest of the party. 'There's no easy way to say this,' she began, 'but it looks like we've been robbed and, to make matters worse, the bus has been trashed as well. Poppa's tour bag is missing with the gig money, and if you left anything valuable on or around your seats, I doubt it's there now. Before you come on board to check, we need to establish who was last on the bus so that we can work out when all this was happening. It must have taken some time to do this much damage. Tilly and Patty disturbed the cat who did it just now, but we need to know if any of you came back to the bus during the evening, and if you saw anyone hanging around.'

Everyone shook their head and Boobah spoke up. 'What about Suzi? Maybe she made off vith the money.'

Derek scowled at her. 'She wouldn't do that. I know she wouldn't,' he said.

'But how can you know this? It's not the first time tonight that she has done a disappearing act!' shouted Boobah.

Hettie could see that the slanging match was gathering heat and she acted quickly, before everyone started to take sides. 'We're in enough of a mess as it is without turning on each other. As it's your bus, Derek, I think you'd better come aboard first to check the damage. The rest of you need to wait your turn. There's not much room at the moment because of all the stuff that's been chucked everywhere.'

Derek gingerly climbed the steps and took in the detritus, looking to the back of the bus which was, after all, his home. He let out a pitiful howl, and Hettie watched as he made his way down the aisle, stepping over the mess as he went. There were even bigger casualties than his slashed bed and cushions: his paintings had been destroyed, the canvases ripped from one corner to another, and his oil paint tubes squeezed out all over the floor. He stood and cried, his shoulders lifting and falling with every sob.

Poppa rose from his seat to comfort him. Hettie started to collect together some of the clothes and bags in the gangway, putting them all on the front seat for the cats to sort through and reclaim. 'I'm afraid this one has Belisha written all over it, Derek mate,' Poppa said, as the cat tried to control himself. 'I reckon she's got it in for you all right.'

Derek shook his head. 'I just can't believe she'd do this. Maybe to me, but not to the rest of the cats on the tour. I can believe she'd wreck my paintings, but taking money and trashing the bus – why would she do that?'

'Maybe you've become a little too successful with your magic act,' suggested Hettie. 'You went down a storm tonight, and it's clear that Magical Mystery Paws could really go places with a few more tricks and a bit more polish.'

'That's all thanks to Suzi,' Derek said. 'She's running the show, really. She worked out the saw trick and the card stuff.'

'Well, I think under the circumstances we need to find Suzi,' said Hettie. 'We've got a lynch mob on our paws out there and, just for the record, she needs to have a believable alibi.'

Derek began to collect his things, looking for items to salvage. He hauled his mattress back onto the bed, turning it upside down to hide the slash marks. The coloured cushions were past saving, along with the tubes of paint and most of the canvases, which he put in a pile ready to take off the bus.

Tilly reappeared, sporting two perfectly bandaged front paws but looking none the worse for her ordeal. 'They're getting a bit nasty out there,' she said.

'I suppose we'd better let a few of them on now that things are looking slightly better. Is there any sign of Suzi?'

Tilly shook her head. 'No, but they think she robbed us, because she told Boobah in Felix Toe that she was absolutely broke and owed some of her friends money. She'd promised to pay it back at the end of the tour, evidently.'

'That *is* interesting, but Poppa thinks that Belisha Beacon is at the bottom of this one. We shouldn't rule Suzi out, though, and Deirdre was late for supper, too. If you're feeling up to it, let's see if we can find Suzi. Deirdre said that she left her at one of those shacks on the beach. If she's still there, she's in the clear.'

'Sounds like a good plan,' said Poppa, turning Tilly's tartan shopper the right way up and putting it on her seat. 'I'll oversee things here and carry on sorting the bus out. Maybe I'll find my gig bag somewhere. I just can't get my head round all that missing money. I was so stupid to leave it all in one place – and that bag's got all the tour contracts and venue info in it as well... Although, I doubt we'll be going any further than home at this rate. At least I've got the gig money from tonight still in my pocket.'

'And Marley took loads of money on the T-shirts, too,' said Tilly brightly. 'She's got it in her truck. I helped her count it.'

Hettie felt for Poppa. He'd tried so hard to make the tour work and it had risen from the ashes time after time – after Alice's death, followed swiftly by Patty's fall, and now a robbery and the destruction of Derek's bus. She owed it to him to get to the bottom of the crimes and discover who had set out to derail the tour; whoever it was, it looked like they had succeeded.

'Where are we supposed to be tomorrow?' she asked, trying to remember where she'd left her tour list.

'Lowerslop Pier, but I don't see the point in taking this any further.'

It was Derek who spoke next. 'If you chuck the tour now, whoever is doing this will have won. If we can catch them, we might at least get the money back.'

'And what if it ends up being Belisha?' said Hettie.

'Then she'll get what's coming to her. I just hope Suzi's not involved. She told *me* she was broke, too, but I wouldn't have her down as a thief, and certainly not a vandal.'

'Well, we'll see if we can find her,' said Hettie. She turned on her heel and set out for the dunes with Tilly, leaving the rest of the company to sort through their belongings on the bus.

Patty sat silently in the seat that Poppa had found for her, sniffing the air and moving her head from side to side.

Chapter Twenty-Two

At night the dunes were a magical place. The shacks, which were so stark in daylight, became little encampments of light and music, and the sound of guitars and whistles drifted across the sand. The holidaymakers were making the most of their freedom from the mundane grind of everyday life, living out every moment under the sun and stars. The moon was almost full and cut a silver pathway across the sea, which had come closer to the land, as if searching for something.

'Deirdre said that the shack where Suzi stopped was over this giant ridge of sand,' explained Hettie, looking down on the scene, as Tilly puffed her way up the dune. 'It could be one of three as far as I can see, so take your pick.'

Catching her breath, Tilly surveyed the shacks at the bottom of the ridge. 'I think we should start in the middle – the one with all those lovely candles. There's definitely music coming from there.'

Hettie agreed and helped Tilly down onto the flat sand, fearing that if she fell, she would hurt her bandaged paws. Outside, the shack was a hive of activity. Two cats strummed guitars while another tended a make-shift barbecue – and several more sprawled on cushions, smoking catnip, one with a tiny kitten asleep in her arms. At a glance, there was no sign of Suzi. Hettie felt awkward at disturbing such an idyllic scene, but the whereabouts of the guitarist was vital and the sooner she was found, the sooner she could be dismissed from the case – or at least from the robbery. She adopted a no-nonsense approach, addressing the cat by the barbe-cue. 'I'm sorry to disturb you, but we're looking for a friend of ours. Suzi Quake?'

'Yeah, right,' said the cat, poised with a sausage on the end of her fork. 'She went to borrow a box so we could do some stuff. Yer know, hang out a bit, blow some smoke. Her band's done a gig in the village.'

'You say she went to borrow a guitar – how long ago was that?'

'Hard to say. Maybe one hour, maybe two. Time just drifts out here. Maybe she got involved with another scene and changed her mind. No pressure.'

Hettie was a little frustrated by the maybes and tried another approach. 'Do you know Suzi very well?'

One of the male cats with a guitar stopped playing and stood up to speak. 'You're beginning to sound like one of those detectives. Why the questions? You can see she's not here. We're just having a peaceful time, and Suzi's not the sort of cat who needs a minder. If you're friends of hers you should know that, so why don't you leave us in peace? Because right now you're crashing in on some special time.'

He had a point. The scene they'd created was a beautiful one, and Hettie would have been more than happy to join them if she hadn't been on official business. At least they now knew that Suzi had no alibi, and that put her firmly in the frame for the robbery. Making their apologies, Hettie and Tilly walked on towards the sea, not wanting to return to the chaos of the bus before they had to.

'This case is a bloody nightmare,' observed Hettie, as they stared out across the water. 'The systematic trashing of Derek's bus has Belisha's spiteful style about it, but as far as we know she's still walking the cliffs at West Grunting.'

'Unless Derek shoved her off,' said Tilly.

'Judging by the way everyone has behaved on this tour, that's a distinct possibility and I wouldn't blame him. But Belisha *did* return to the bus to collect her things after their row – unless Derek dumped them, of course.'

'So why didn't she mess the bus up then? Why wait until tonight?'

'You're right,' agreed Hettie. 'That was the perfect moment to strike back at Derek and mess up a tour that she was no longer part of. When you come to think of it, that bus has been a battleground of sorts right from the start: Belisha jealously guarding her space, Suzi and Deirdre's slanging matches, Patty's fall – and now all this tonight. What about the cat who shoved you? Did you get even a glimpse?'

Tilly looked down at her injured paws, trying to remember the exact sequence of events. 'It was all so quick,' she said. 'I remember seeing the bus in darkness. The door was open, so I climbed up the steps and felt for the switch that works the emergency lights – Bruiser showed me it the other day after Patty's fall. Then something hit me so fast that I lost my balance and fell out of the bus. I don't think I touched the steps on the way down. I tried to save myself with my paws but my face went down, and whoever it was trod on the back of my head as if they were using me for a springboard.'

'Did they feel heavy or light?' Hettie asked.

'Hard to say,' said Tilly. 'It was all so quick.'

'Well, unless she's returned to the village hall, we can definitely say that Suzi Quake is missing,' said Hettie, trying to be decisive. 'It would make sense for her to run away if she's stolen the tour money.'

'But what about Deirdre? We know she could have pushed Patty off the bus at Felix Toe. She was missing for most of suppertime tonight and she left us packing up to go off with Suzi. She can't have knocked me off the bus because she was at Marley's truck then, but if Suzi and Deirdre are in this together, they could have planned the robbery between them. So maybe it was Suzi who knocked me down the steps?'

'Or Belisha, if she's still at large. Or it could easily be one of the good cats of Wobbleswick, snatching an opportunity while we were all at supper. Or maybe Agnes Leek is a cat burglar by night. On the face of it, what happened tonight could have nothing to do with anything that's gone before,' Hettie concluded, suddenly becoming despondent.

The two cats walked along the seashore in silence, both wanting to get as far away from the case as possible but realising that the responsibility of finding a solution was becoming more urgent than ever. Alice was dead, Patty had come close and there was no reason to dismiss the idea that the killer could strike again. Reluctantly, they retraced their steps, giving the shack cats a wide berth so as not to intrude any further. They reached the village hall in time to see Bruiser and Flaky packing all the gear and instruments into the hold. Derek was directing them, making sure that his magic box was safely stowed away – although it would be of little use if Suzi failed to return before the bus left for Lowerslop in the morning.

The bus looked considerably better, with everyone making the best of things. Poppa's tour bag had turned up, shoved under one of the seats at the front of the bus; the paperwork for the tour was still inside, but the money was nowhere to be found. There was a pile of clothes on Hettie's seat, put there in a process of elimination by Poppa after the rest of the cats had claimed their belongings. Hettie was pleased to see her T-shirts, and Tilly was especially delighted to see her new poncho on top of the pile.

Tilly suddenly remembered her bingo winnings and rushed to her tartan shopper, lifting the flap at the front with one of her bandaged paws. 'Ooh, look!' she said. 'I've still got my twenty pounds – the robber missed that. Here you are, Poppa – you can have this. It might help a bit.'

Poppa waved the money away but appreciated the sentiment. Marley had already handed over the T-shirt money, and the door takings had been very good at the village hall; if the rest of the tour went ahead as planned, it was still possible to break even, but who would play the next gig? Lowerslop was the centre of the universe as far as punk music was concerned. It was the first gig that Poppa had booked, and the cat who did the promotions for the pier amusement centre – known locally as Bondage Pete – was a huge Patty Sniff fan. Audiences would travel from as far away as Pidley-on-Sea, he'd said. Patty had made a good recovery from her fall, but Poppa knew that it was a very big ask to expect her to get back on stage so soon – and without Suzi they were now short of a bass player; if she'd scarpered with the tour money, she'd be long gone.

The tour had become fraught with ifs and buts: the only certainty was that everyone was exhausted from their night's work, both performing and clearing up the aftermath of the robbery. Poppa announced that he would decide in the morning what was best, and the tour party settled down to sleep in the hope that a new day would bring with it a clear and positive direction.

Tilly tried to sleep, but her sore paws were keeping her awake. To pass the time, she reached awkwardly for Alice's Filofax, which was in the front flap of her shopper –as the sun began to rise, everything became clear to her. If her theory was right, Suzi Quake was in grave danger. Tilly was tempted to wake Hettie and share her ideas but then thought better of it; she had no concrete evidence to support her theory and, if she was right, they had made a serious error of judgement in their investigations so far. She finally fell into a deep sleep and woke with a start as Marley Toke announced that breakfast was being served at her truck.

Boobah was first off the bus when Bruiser and Flaky put her ramp in place, and she was pleased to get right across the car park without stopping. Kitty and her dancers were next, all keen to see what delights Marley had in store. The smell of fish filled the air, as the Jamaican cook filled her griddle with a whole shoal of sardines, which she'd bartered for by the small jetty close to the village that morning. Derek, who'd woken early, had appointed himself breakfast assistant and was busy laying out the plates and cutting up the bread as the sardines sizzled.

Hettie struggled awake, feeling completely unrefreshed after a sleep peppered with beach shacks, dead cats and several appearances from Agnes Leek. She'd slept awkwardly, and her neck and back were stiff and sore. As she came to, the recollection of her stage triumph was way down the list of memories to carry into a new day. She pulled herself up to peer over the seats, hoping to see Suzi safely returned to the fold, but there was no sign of her.

Tilly was still sleepy in the seat behind – not at all her usual bright morning self. Hettie moved to sit next to her. 'It's not like you to be still asleep. Are your paws hurting?'

Tilly nodded, looking washed out after her night with Alice Slap's Filofax. She was tempted to share her findings with Hettie there and then, but Poppa scuppered the opportunity by swinging into the seat opposite. 'I bring good news and bad,' he began. 'Suzi is a no-show, so it looks like we're short of a bass player – which is a sod, as Patty just told me that she's ready to get back on stage and is keen to do the gig tonight. We really do need the money, so I'm tempted to let her. I'm off to breakfast to see if Tarmac – or even Moya, Aisling or Kitty – can handle the bass that Suzi was kind enough to leave behind. With the sort of money she's made off with, she'll be able to buy a much more expensive bit of gear.' The last comment was made through tightly gritted teeth, and Poppa left the bus in search of another honorary Cheese Triangle.

Tilly was about to discuss her suspicions once again with Hettie, but this time it was Patty who demanded attention. Her voice from the back of the bus sounded urgent. 'Hey, Tilly – are you there? I could do with some help. I need to find some clean stuff to wear and I'm starving.' Tilly responded as a good minder should and pulled on a clean T-shirt before going to Patty's aid. Hettie decided to stick with yesterday's clothes for travelling and went to join the breakfast queue at Marley's truck, noticing as she passed that Deirdre was still fast asleep on her seat.

Except for the bandage, Patty looked her old self. Derek had been kind enough to let her sleep on his mattress once again, and the rest had obviously done her good. Tilly pawed through Patty's small suitcase, describing the possibilities to her. 'You've got clean black, blue and purple T-shirts, as well as a white one with "Stuff You!" on the front.'

Patty put her head on one side, thinking about her audience. 'I think I'll save the "Stuff You!" for the gig. What does the purple one say?'

Tilly held the T-shirt up and was slightly shocked by the slogan. Before she had time to read it out, Patty made up her mind. 'Yeah, that'll do. Purple's good, and I'll probably end up spilling my breakfast down it. Great comment, though.'

Tilly was too tired to read anything into Patty's words and left her to dress, promising to return to take her to breakfast. She was in desperate need of a mug of milky tea. She passed Deirdre, still fast asleep in her seat, and was tempted to wake her but her paws were throbbing and she needed Marley to look at them to make sure that they were healing properly.

When Deirdre Nightshade was satisfied that she and Patty were the only cats left on the bus, she sat up, rubbing her eyes with her paws. She could see that Patty was busy getting dressed so she took the opportunity to stand on her seat and reach up into the luggage rack for her make-up case. She pulled it down and opened it. Inside – covering a multitude of lipsticks, eyeliners and claw varnishes – was a bundle of notes, more money than Deirdre had ever seen. Somewhat reluctantly, she gathered the notes together in her paws and stuffed them all under Poppa's seat. Without a word to Patty, she left the bus to join the others for breakfast.

What Deirdre didn't realise was that Patty Sniff had made a full recovery in every sense of the word. Patty watched as the blurred images became clear in more ways than one: how strange that the tour should not only bring her music career back, but also her sight. As she sat waiting for Tilly, the tears rolled down her face; they were tears of joy, but tinged with sadness at the new world she'd just entered. Who was the cat she'd seen putting money under a seat, and what did it all mean? She needed Tilly more than ever to introduce her to the strangers whose voices she knew and whose faces were waiting to be identified. For now, though, she would keep her secret, as she knew it was probably a dangerous one. She dried her eyes on the hem of her purple T-shirt, put her dark glasses on and made her way to the front of the bus to wait for Tilly to fetch her.

Chapter Twenty-Three

The weary travellers had formed an orderly queue at Marley's hatch to receive their sardines. Hettie and Poppa – claiming seniority – had pushed to the front of the queue and were sitting in the morning sunshine, enjoying their breakfast. Tilly joined them, having received some of Marley's 'magical all-purpose cream' for her paws. Within minutes they'd stopped hurting and, although the cream's ingredients were a secret that Marley would carry to her grave, Tilly was willing to bet that catnip was involved. 'Have you sorted a bass player yet?' she asked, as Poppa chewed his way through a sardine and left Hettie to reply.

'No. It would seem that Kitty's dance troupe are not au fait with bass guitars, although Aisling has stepped forward to be Derek's latest assistant – much to Boobah's annoyance – so at least we have a magic act of sorts. Derek *does* seem to work his way through the female cat population at an alarming rate.'

Tilly resisted a giggle, feeling that it wasn't entirely appropriate, and went to collect Patty for breakfast. She was waiting at the front of the bus, keen to join the rest of the party. 'I can smell that fish from here,' she said. 'I've suddenly got me appetite back, and I'm really looking forward to the gig tonight. Any sign of Suzi?'

'No, I'm afraid not,' Tilly said, steering Patty towards the sardines. 'Poppa's asked the dancers, but none of them can play a bass guitar.'

'Well, that settles it,' said Patty. 'I'll just have to do it meself. It's a long time since I picked up a bass, but I used to play one in my first band – couldn't afford players in those days, so we used to go out as a three-piece. More money to share out, too.'

Tilly was amazed at the singer's resilience. In spite of her blindness and how many times life had knocked her down, Patty Sniff just kept on going.

They were the last to be served breakfast, so Marley filled their plates – and her own – and escaped her field kitchen to sit with them in the sun, leaving Derek to wash up and Flaky to dry. Patty looked round, finding the light through her dark glasses almost too painful to deal with, but it was a revelation to put faces to voices. She noticed that the cat she'd seen hiding money on the bus was sitting outside Marley's truck, hugging a mug of tea; comparing her with the rest of the cats, it was clear that she was looking at Deirdre Nightshade, her lead guitarist. She looked at Tilly, able to study her face for the first time; she was older and smaller than Patty had imagined, but there was a warmth about her eyes and her small twitching ears that was endearing and made her seem so approachable. Suddenly, she felt bad about not sharing her secret with Tilly and decided to put things straight as soon as she could.

Poppa interrupted her thoughts, and she waited for the black-and-white cat to speak as he stood in front of her. 'I'm a bit stuck for a bass player for tonight,' he admitted. 'There's no sign of Suzi, so I wondered if you had any numbers I could call? Maybe someone you've played with in the past?'

Tilly giggled. '*We've* found one, haven't we, Patty?' she said conspiratorially.

'Yeah,' responded Patty. 'Ideal, really. She knows all my stuff and she's free to do the gig tonight.'

'That's brilliant!' Poppa said. 'Do we need to pick her up from anywhere?'

This time Patty laughed. 'No. I'm sitting right here.'

It took Poppa a minute to grasp the situation; when he did, his face was filled with concern rather than triumph. 'I'm amazed you're happy to sing after what you've been through, let alone haul a heavy bass on stage as well. Are you sure you'll be okay?'

Patty smiled, showing a set of very white teeth. 'You can't keep a good 'un down, as my old ma used to say – and we've got some albums to shift.'

Poppa was delighted that yet another problem set to destroy the tour had been averted, and he still had every hope that Suzi might return to vindicate herself from the robbery. He left a note pinned to the door of the village hall, telling her where they were going, but time was ticking on and he'd arranged to meet Bondage Pete by Lowerslop Pier at one o'clock.

On Poppa's instruction, Bruiser pulled Suzi's bass guitar out of the luggage store, and Patty settled down on Derek's bed to familiarise herself with the instrument. She insisted that Tilly sit with her on the journey, hoping for a chance to share her secret. Tilly had intended to share some secrets of her own with Hettie, but as everything was now moving towards the next performance, she decided to bide her time. There were a couple of conversations to be had before she laid out her theory, but Patty was her priority at the moment.

Seeing that Tilly was otherwise occupied, Hettie decided to sit with Deirdre, hoping to carry out some investigations of her own while Bruiser allowed the bus to meander along the coastal road to Lowerslop. 'Did Suzi say anything to you last night about leaving the tour?' she began.

Deirdre looked a little taken aback by Hettie's direct question, but responded as best she could. 'Not really, although we did talk about forming our own band eventually. She said the magic act was a bit of fun, but she wasn't serious about it.'

'And what about Derek?' asked Hettie. 'Was she serious about him?'

Deirdre shrugged her bony shoulders. 'I doubt it. He's got a reputation for loving them and leaving them, and Suzi wouldn't want to get into all that. She's a bit of a flirt, but she gets bored easily.'

'How long have you known Derek, then?' said Hettie, trying to keep things casual.

'Well, he's one of those cats you just *know*, if you know what I mean. He seems to pop up everywhere.'

Hetty was intrigued to find out more about where Derek might have popped up, when Derek himself popped up from the seat in front, where he'd been dozing. 'Got a roll-up you could spare?' he asked. 'I'm out of papers, but I've got a tin of catnip.'

Deirdre passed over her liquorice papers. 'Yeah, here you go – and you can roll one for me while you're at it.' Hettie was tempted to fetch her pipe and join them, but she needed to keep a clear head. She decided to sit with Poppa for the rest of the journey to talk about the plans for the next gig.

Tilly watched, fascinated, as Patty's claws shot up and down the bass guitar's fretboard as if she'd been born to it. Although there was no clear sound in its unplugged state, Tilly could hear enough to know that Patty had got the hang of the instrument very quickly. When she'd worked through the songs for Lowerslop, Patty put the bass to one side. 'Are you any good at keeping secrets?' she whispered in Tilly's direction. Tilly loved a secret and responded by shuffling closer to Patty on the bed, having no idea what was coming. 'The thing is,' Patty began, keeping her voice down, 'that bang on the head made me feel a bit weird – flashing lights and all that stuff. When the headache wore off, everything went a bit fuzzy instead of black, which is what I'm used to. Then we surprised that cat on the bus after the gig last night, and I thought I could see a shape as they ran off.'

Tilly was transfixed and held her breath as Patty continued. 'Then this morning, when you were sorting through my T-shirts, I could read the slogan on the purple one and I knew for sure what was happening.'

Tilly managed to suppress her excitement. All she really wanted to do was dance down the gangway of the bus in sheer joy at what Patty was telling her, but it was a secret and she would have to behave herself. 'You mean you can see?' she whispered.

'Yeah, but I'm not ready for anyone to know yet. I'm finding it really strange and it's freaking me out a bit, but I didn't want to keep it from you, as you've been really great with me. I thought if you could play along with the blind thing for a bit, I could try and get used to things in my own good time. I don't want any fuss, and it might even be dangerous.'

'Why dangerous?' asked Tilly, still trying to digest the news.

'Because cats behave differently if they think you're blind. They do things in front of you as if there was no one else there.'

Tilly was a little confused, but pushed on. 'You said you saw a shape when I got pushed down the bus steps – what sort of shape? Thin, fat, tall, short?'

Patty thought for a moment before replying. 'More round than anything. And afterwards Alice's perfume was on the bus again, but that wasn't the worst of it: I saw something this morning, when you went to get your paws seen to, which could be a bit difficult for us all.'

Tilly was intrigued and bursting to find out, but the bus lurched into a car park close to Lowerslop Pier. Suddenly, everyone was on their feet, collecting their things together, and keen to see what a new venue and a new town had to offer. Patty took one of Tilly's injured paws and squeezed it gently. 'Please keep my secret for a bit longer. I'm not ready to face up to this yet.'

Tilly nodded, knowing that she would have to share the good news with Hettie as soon as she could, but she was still desperate to find out what Patty had seen that morning. The clamour on the bus made the conversation impossible – and as the day unfolded, there was much worse to come than the actions of a petty thief.

* * *

Bondage Pete stood out like a sore claw. The shaved fur on the top of his head, as well as the rings and safety pins that punctured his nose and ears, signalled very clearly to Poppa that he was a punk cat through and through. Pete had run the Lowerslop Pier venue for some years, offering family entertainment by day and radical music bands in the evenings. He'd become a promoter after his own band, Bleach Bondage, had split up due to irreconcilable differences. The fights had left the dressing room and taken centre stage during the band's performances, and Pete – after a nasty slashing with a razor blade – decided to pack up as soon as the bleeding had stopped. He came from a long succession of entertainers and showcats: his grandfather had travelled the length and breadth of the seaside piers with his music-hall act, and his father had started the ice rink and amusement arcade at Moggs Eye beach near Skegmess, before fatally injuring himself on the penny-a-shot rifle range. Inheriting his family's eye for an act to pull in the crowds, Pete had made a real go of Loweslop Pier and was ecstatic when Poppa called him to offer Patty Sniff for the venue.

'I'm afraid you'll have to cart your gear right to the end of the pier,' he said by way of a greeting. 'We used to have a steam train that ran along here, which was great for getting stuff in, but the old cat who ran it forgot to apply the brakes and the whole thing went straight off and into the drink. Forty passengers all swimming for their lives, mostly kittens. You've got to laugh, haven't you?'

Poppa wasn't too sure about Pete's sense of humour, but one look at the length of the pier told him that they needed to get on with the unloading. Summoning Bruiser, Flaky and Derek, he set to hauling the gear out of the hold. Poppa enlisted the help of his sack barrow to wheel some of the amplifiers, and Flaky and Bruiser lifted the speakers between them. Derek stayed with the bus, pulling out instruments and flight cases, ready for Poppa's return. Led by Hettie, the rest of the tour company set out along the pier for the venue, with Patty staying close to Tilly, as she always did.

The hall had a tall, domed ceiling and had clearly been quite something when it was first built, but weather and a lack of money had turned this end of the pier into a rather shabby shadow of its former self. There were buckets placed on the floor wherever the roof above had given in to the North Sea storms that lashed the coastline, although they were currently dry due to the hot weather. The venue itself smelt of stale beer and catnip, and the floor – unlike the one in Agnes Leek's village hall – was smeared where a mop had half-heartedly been dragged across it. There was a bar at one end, where a cat was busy changing barrels and stocking up on crisps.

Bondage Pete showed no sign of offering to help in getting the gear in. He was keener to be introduced to Patty, but Tilly had protectively steered her backstage in the hope of finding a dressing room. The backstage area was much nicer than the hall, mainly because it had been done up to accommodate a kittens' holiday workshop. Several areas were decorated in bright colours, and furnished with beanbags and cushions, and a series of large mirrors reflected the light. The windows looked directly out to sea, and Patty forgot herself to marvel at the view; luckily, the rest of the party was too far behind to notice her delight, although Tilly did wonder just how long they could keep the charade going.

Tarmac wheeled Boobah the length of the pier and settled her in a comfortable spot backstage before returning to the bus to fetch Enya's keyboard. The rest of the dancers gathered round her for a pre-gig pep talk, although Cormac excused himself to set up Alice's drum kit. Bondage Pete finally broke through to the backstage area and swooped on Patty. He was totally star-struck, and Tilly was impressed by her monosyllabic punk star attitude towards him. In a normal situation, Patty's coolness could have been interpreted as rude, but she knew that an off-paw manner was expected of her and Pete was lapping it up. Tilly decided to return to the bus to change. She'd made up her mind to treat herself to a 'Summer of Fluff' official tour T-shirt, and she was also keen to find out what Marley had planned for dinner. The sardines had been served some time ago, and in their hurry to get the gear in, no one had mentioned lunch. The Butters' paper bags were long gone, and Tilly was seriously considering a shopping trip to stock up on treats.

Hettie, Derek and Poppa were unloading the magic box when she got back to the bus, and Hettie's language wasn't exactly family-friendly as she took hold of one end, trying with Derek to haul it onto the sack barrow while Poppa held it steady. 'You need a bloody crane to lift this, Derek. It needs wheels – or, better still, an engine so you can drive it to gigs,' she said. 'And it smells like you've got an out-of-date chicken in there. Are you storing your laundry in it?'

Hettie was right. As Tilly came closer to the magic box, the smell coming from the knife slits was almost unbearable. The box was finally upended onto the sack barrow and Poppa started to wheel it forward, with Derek and Hettie hanging onto the sides. They'd only gone a few yards across the car park before the door flew open and the magic box revealed its latest trick. Suzi Quake had been stabbed repeatedly and lay in a shroud of her own congealed blood. The flies that buzzed round her body were the only sign of life, and it was clear that she'd been dead for some time. Poppa, Hettie and Derek lowered the box back onto the ground, too stunned to utter anything. Tilly stood a little distance away, fighting back the nausea in the summer heat. The flies, even though they'd been released from their tomb, continued their dance of death around the corpse.

Poppa was the first to speak, and predictably said the first thing that came into his head: 'No wonder it was so heavy.'

Marley had been watching the commotion from her truck and came over to see if she could help or offer a cheerful word of encouragement. She froze as she peered into the magic box. 'Oh my days! Dis is just de worst ting I seen in me whole life. What sorta cat can do dis to anodder cat?'

Marley had voiced everyone's thoughts, and Poppa gently closed the box.

Chapter Twenty-Four

Hettie Bagshot decided to take control. So far, she'd allowed the case to meander along the coastal road with Derek's bus, picking up the odd snippet of evidence on the way without any meaningful breakthroughs. After the discovery of Suzi Quake's body, it was clear that the tour must come to an end – out of decency, if not necessity – but Hettie knew that if the Lowerslop gig went ahead, there just might be a chance to catch the killer, who was doing his or her best to bring the Summer of Fluff Tour to a premature and bloody conclusion. After putting Derek's magic box back in the luggage hold, Hettie, Tilly and Poppa adjourned to the bus, leaving Derek and Marley to comfort each other. Hettie had sworn them to silence about their gruesome discovery, and she locked the door behind her so that her crisis meeting would not be disturbed.

'Right,' said Hettie, as Tilly and Poppa found seats close to her. 'Let's try and sort this mess out. First we need to get rid of Suzi's body. We can't carry it around in this heat, so I suggest we put in a call to Morbid Balm and get her to do what she calls a "removal". She could be here in an hour and have Suzi tucked up in one of her fridges by dinner time.'

Poppa and Tilly nodded their heads in agreement.

'Next,' Hettie continued, 'we need to decide about the gig tonight. I think if we cancel it, we'll be playing into the killer's paws. If we go ahead, they may reveal themselves – but we need to box clever. There's no point in upsetting everyone with the news of Suzi's death, if we can get Morbid to be discreet over her collection. The killer is probably assuming that we'll make the discovery closer to show time, which I think must be their plan. If *I* were the killer, I'd want to be around to see that happen – so we must all be nonchalant and vigilant at the same time.'

Poppa and Tilly nodded again, pleased to have Hettie's steady paw at the tiller.

'Poppa, I think you should get back to the hall as if nothing has happened and carry on with the setting up. You'll have to let Bruiser know what's going on, as we'll need him to keep his eyes peeled. Derek should come with you and rehearse Aisling in as if the magic act is going ahead. They'll have to stick with card tricks for now until the box is free – we need to pretend that everything is normal.'

Poppa stood up to leave and Hettie followed him off the bus, telling Tilly to stay put while she phoned Morbid. She returned ten minutes later with her mission accomplished, two large ham baps and two mugs of milky tea, rustled up for them by Marley as the perfect working lunch. While she was waiting, Tilly had prepared the evidence required to put forward her theory, which – after Suzi's death – seemed more plausible than ever. It was time for all the secrets to be offered up before another cat was hurt.

Marley was on patrol in the car park, looking out for Morbid, so Hettie and Tilly settled themselves on Derek's bed, where they could spread out and enjoy their lunch. They were both hungry and made short work of the baps, washing them down with the tea. Refreshed and ready to pull in the pieces of the giant jigsaw before them, Tilly spoke first. 'I'm not sure where to start,' she said, 'but I've got a theory and a secret to tell you.'

'Let's start with the secret,' said Hettie. 'I'm all ears.'

Tilly brushed some crumbs from her T-shirt and sat up straight, ready to offer her important information. 'It's a good-news secret, really,' she began. 'Patty has got her sight back. It must have been her bang on the head that did it. It's been fuzzy at first, but now she can see properly, but she doesn't want anyone to know because she says that cats act differently if they think you can't see, and that could be dangerous. And she's already seen something. And she thinks the cat who pushed me down the steps was round. And every time something bad happens, she can smell Alice Slap's perfume.'

Tilly took a deep breath, and Hettie tried to make sense of what her friend had just told her. 'So... just to get this straight,' she said. 'Patty can see, but doesn't want anyone to know because she's seen something she shouldn't, which puts her in danger?'

'Yes, that's right, and I think it might have something to do with Deirdre. What she actually said was that she'd seen something that could be "difficult for us all".'

'So what makes you think Deirdre's involved?' asked Hettie, a little confused.

'Because Deirdre was still on the bus with Patty this morning when I went to get my paws fixed. Patty was just about to tell me what she'd seen when we arrived here, and I haven't had a chance to speak to her again since.'

'Well, we obviously need to know what she saw, so I'll leave that one with you – but what about this round cat who knocked you over? What did she mean by that? It obviously wasn't Suzi – she would have been dead by then and tucked up in Derek's box. Perhaps the thief was from Wobbleswick and grabbed an opportunity while the bus was empty? A round cat isn't exactly a description we can nail down to anyone – except perhaps you, me or Marley.'

'Ah, but you haven't heard my theory yet,' said Tilly, reaching for Alice's Filofax and turning to an entry that she'd marked. 'There's a lot of stuff about the recording sessions with Patty, but in April Alice writes: "D has asked me to move in. S says it'll never work and could get in the way of the band." Then there's lots of love stuff and scribbles. The next significant entry is a few weeks later, when they're recording at Tabby Road. She writes: "Meeting D for supper." The next day she writes: "Fed up with this on–off thing. Really getting to me. She's moved into my space." Then a couple of weeks later she says: "Looks like the tour's on. Thinking of jumping ship now. I just can't face seeing D every day. She's really got it coming to her." And then, finally, the last entry before she died: "Hacked off. D hardly said a word. Sick of pretending."'

Hettie had been listening carefully to Tilly's pick of Alice Slap's diary entries, but was still none the wiser. 'Okay,' she said, 'but all this tells us is what we know already: Alice formed an attachment to Deirdre, and Deirdre put a stop to it.'

Tilly shook her head. 'Not necessarily,' she said. 'It's all this stuff about "she's moved into my space" and "she's got it coming to her". If D doesn't stand for Deirdre, it could easily stand for…'

'Derek!' shouted Hettie.

'Yes,' said Tilly. 'If you read Derek every time she writes a D, it all makes perfect sense. Alice had a fling with Derek, and then *she* moved into her space, "she" being…'

'Belisha bloody Beacon!' said Hettie. 'Well, if you're right, this whole mess revolves around her and there's no reason why she shouldn't strike again. She seems to be bumping off anyone who shows the slightest interest in Derek, and she's clearly following the tour. Derek, and now Aisling, are at risk. We need to set a trap, and there's no time to lose. Well done! A brilliant piece of detection, if I may say so, although Derek could have been a little more helpful. If he'd owned up to knowing Alice, Suzi might still be alive. Deirdre has some explaining to do, as well. We need to double-check your theory and ask Derek outright if he was seeing Alice. You'll also have to find out from Patty if it *was* Deirdre she saw.'

Tilly was pleased that Hettie had praised her theory, but now they must bring the Summer of Fluff case – as it would forever be known – to its inevitable conclusion before the body count increased.

Chapter Twenty-Five

As Hettie and Tilly left the bus, Morbid Balm pulled into the car park in her van. Hettie directed her to park next to the bus on the far side, by the hold, hoping that the removal would be as discreet as possible. Morbid sprang out from the driver's seat, looking as cheerful as ever, and approached Hettie, rubbing her paws together. 'So wotcha got for me this fine sunny day?' she asked.

'Nothing too sunny, I'm afraid,' replied Hettie. 'But we're very pleased to see you. This one's a bit messy.'

Morbid smiled. Almost without exception, the corpses she'd dealt with for the No. 2 Feline Detective Agency had been messy – and she would have been disappointed if they weren't. Morbid took great pride in cleaning up the nastiness of death and sending her customers to their graves looking almost as good as new.

Hettie opened the hold to reveal Derek's magic box. Tilly and Marley took one end, and Morbid and Hettie the other, and between them they managed to wrestle the box onto the floor of the car park, where Hettie lifted the lid to reveal its gory contents. 'I see what you mean,' said Morbid, batting away the flies with her paw. 'This one's a bit ripe, too. Nice box, though – was she a magic trick that went wrong?'

Hettie admired Morbid's down-to-earth attitude; nothing seemed to faze her. 'You could say that,' she said, 'but there's a lot more to it.'

'If you two are involved, there usually is. Do you want me to take her away in the box?'

Hettie shook her head. 'No, we need the box. Have you got anything to put her in?'

Morbid moved towards the back of her van. 'No worries. I've brought a collapsible with me.'

Hettie, Tilly and Marley stared as Morbid hauled a long piece of cardboard out and laid it on the ground next to the magic box. She pulled on the sides and the cardboard responded by forming a perfect, cat-sized coffin. Morbid secured the shape by shooting several small bolts into place and stood back to admire her work. 'Right,' she said. 'This is the sticky bit. Who's going to grab her feet?'

Tilly and Marley backed away, leaving Hettie as the only candidate. Wanting to get it over with as quickly as possible, she moved to Suzi's feet and grabbed her Doc Martens, as Morbid lifted her head. With one movement, the body was transferred to the makeshift coffin and the four cats lifted it into the back of Morbid's van. The flies were still in attendance, so Morbid reached for an aerosol can and sprayed it liberally, inviting them to leave for new horizons. She then slid a cardboard lid across her new passenger and slammed the doors shut on Suzi Quake.

'I'll take her back to Shroud and Trestle, and clean her up. Is there a next of kin we should contact?'

Hettie shook her head, realising that she knew nothing about Susie Quake's life beyond The Cheese Triangles. 'She was the bass player in Patty Sniff's backing band,' Hettie explained. 'Perhaps Patty or Deirdre knows more about her. The thing is, I can't ask them at the moment because I don't want them to know she's dead. I promise I'll ask as soon as I can – maybe after the gig tonight.'

'So Patty's doing a gig here tonight?' said Morbid. 'I'd quite like to hang around and see that, if you can get me in. I've got nothing booked in back at base until tomorrow, and if I put the refrigeration unit on in my van, she'll stay cool enough until later. Knowing you lot, the body count might have risen by then.'

Morbid obviously meant her comment as a joke, but Hettie and Tilly shared a look that suggested she was much closer to the mark than she could imagine. 'Of course we can get you in,' said Hettie. 'It's the least we can do. We're going to the hall now if you want to come with us, but you'll have to make out that you've come especially for the gig – we're keeping this death under wraps for the time being.'

'No problem,' said Morbid. 'I'll park the van over there and head off for a walk first, though. It's ages since I've been to the seaside, and I might just treat myself to a poke of chips and a few rays on the beach before the gig.' She moved the van to a discreet area of the car park; it carried no signage, and the only clue to its gruesome cargo was the spinning vent in the roof, which every fresh- and frozen-food van was equipped with.

Marley returned to her truck to prepare the evening meal for the tour party. She was making her special fish stew with Jamaican dumplings – a comfort food to which she turned in times of crisis. Hettie and Tilly hauled Derek's much lighter but bloodied magic box back into the hold for Poppa to collect later, locked the bus and set off along the pier to the hall.

The place was a hive of activity: Bruiser and Flaky were wiring the stage; Poppa was setting up his mixing desk; Cormac was practising some high leaps under Boobah's instruction; Kitty, Moya, Tarmac and Aisling were doing cat power flow yoga, sitting cross-pawed on the floor by the stage; and Patty and Deirdre were working through some chord sequences in some of the new songs. The only cat doing nothing was Derek, who sat on a chair, looking pale and forlorn.

Hettie nudged Tilly and whispered in her ear. 'Now's our chance. Let's have a little chat with Derek and test out your theory. There are some tea things backstage – we'll take him there.'

Hettie signalled to Derek, who seemed happy to leave the tour party for some peace and quiet. Tilly busied herself making cups of tea in the small kitchen, while the other two cats settled themselves on one of the brightly coloured sofas. Derek sat staring at his feet, and Hettie waded in with her enquiries. 'Things, as you know, have taken a turn for the worse, Derek – and I should tell you that Tilly and I are detectives. Since Alice Slap's death, we've been trying to find out who killed her.'

Psycho Derek shot his head up and looked Hettie full in the face. 'What do you mean who killed her? She choked, didn't she?'

Hettie could see the shock on Derek's face and continued. 'Yes, Alice did choke – but not on a bacon sandwich. I'm afraid someone strangled her with a guitar string, and I think it was one of yours.'

This time Derek looked horrified and immediately went on the defensive. 'I don't know how you can say that! I had nothing to do with Alice's death. If it hadn't been for Belisha, we'd still be together. She just crashed in and broke us up. I was so sad when she died. I realised then that I loved her, but Belisha just kept crowding in on me with this magic thing. I was frightened of her, really – she controlled everything I did, including throwing Alice off my bus. We'd only been together a couple of weeks before Belisha made me finish it and moved in herself. She even rubbed Alice's nose in it by stealing her perfume and spraying it all over herself. I know I let Alice down. I wanted to get back with her, but it was all too late and Belisha wouldn't even let me talk to her.' Derek collapsed into floods of tears. His shoulders shook with the sobs, as he was finally able to cry for Alice – and for himself.

Tilly's arrival with three mugs of sweet milky tea was timed to perfection, and she passed a tea towel to Derek so he could blow his nose and dry his eyes. It was with sadness and satisfaction that she'd heard Derek's story, but there was still one question she wanted to ask him, once the crying stopped. 'I'm afraid I peeped at your paintings on the bus before they were ruined,' she confessed. 'There was a portrait just begun, and I wondered who it was?'

Derek took a sip of tea as his eyes filled with tears again. 'It was Alice. I couldn't wait to paint her. I'd been watching them record in Tabby Road – a mate of mine was doing the engineering on Patty's album, and he let me sit in the control box. I did some sketches of Alice then – that's how I met her. I started the portrait the weekend she moved into my bus, but that's as far as it got: just a pencil outline. The story of my life, really.'

Derek stared into his half-drunk tea. Hettie had established all the things that she needed to, but Belisha Beacon was still at large and in a town like Lowerslop it would be like looking for a needle in a haystack. She was convinced that Belisha would show herself before the day was out, and a trap had to be set. She needed Derek to cooperate and behave as if everything was normal, but to do that she had to take him into her confidence. 'Look, Derek,' she began. 'We believe that Belisha murdered Alice. We think she trashed your bus and killed Suzi, as well as striking out at Patty and leaving her for dead. It's clear that she's hell-bent on stopping this tour, which is why we have to put on a great show tonight. If we're right, she won't be able to resist striking again. Suzi is tucked away in Morbid Balm's van, and we're going to fetch the magic box from the bus as if we haven't discovered the body. I'll get Bruiser to clean it up, and then we'll put it on stage ready for your act. You'll start the gig tonight and I'm certain that Belisha will be in the audience to view her handiwork. I'm sure she'd be delighted to watch you reveal a bloody corpse to a live audience – a great way for Magical Mystery Paws to end his career. To make it all work, I want you to start with the disappearing act, with Aisling inside the box, as you come on stage. I want you to make a really big deal of opening the box. We'll be watching for Belisha, and we'll make sure she doesn't escape. I know it's difficult, but we need you to act normally. If Belisha thinks we've discovered Suzi's body already, she may cry off or try to attack you – or Aisling, as she's now your new assistant.'

Derek took in everything that Hettie had to say and began to pull himself together, which was just as well because Bondage Pete walked in on them, looking for Patty. 'I've got a load of punters out there blocking the stage door and wanting Patty's autograph,' he said. 'They won't go away until she shows.'

'She's in the hall with Deirdre,' said Tilly, keen to get rid of the promoter before he heard anything he shouldn't. 'I'll come with you to find her.'

Tilly and Pete left Hettie and Derek, and went back into the hall. It looked as though Patty and Deirdre had finished their rehearsal. Cormac was up on stage, working with Poppa on his drum sound, and Deirdre was waiting to do a soundcheck with her guitar. Pete was pleased to see that Patty was free and made his approach. Tilly marvelled at Patty's lack of reaction as he bore down on her; pretending to be blind was possibly one of her finest performances. Patty was happy for Pete to lead her out to the stage door to meet her fans, so Tilly stayed behind and joined Poppa at the mixing desk, bringing him up to speed on Hettie's master plan and Derek's revelations.

Hettie returned to the hall with Derek, who looked much more in control of himself, and Aisling left the dancers to talk through his act with him. Poppa summoned Bruiser from the lighting box and the two friends set off down the pier to collect Derek's box from the bus, leaving Hettie at the mixing desk in case Patty returned and wanted to do a soundcheck. Deirdre was entertaining the company with a selection of lead guitar solos, which everyone enjoyed, with the exception of Boobah, who sat with her paws over her ears.

The transfer of the magic box was a lot easier without the added weight of a corpse, and Poppa and Bruiser returned quickly with their burden, setting it down in the backstage kitchen. Under Hettie's instructions, Bruiser set about cleaning Suzi Quake's blood from the inside, and before long it was up on stage, looking almost as good as new.

Derek began to shake when he saw the box again. Hettie gave him one of her encouraging but firm looks, and he slunk off to practise his egg-cup trick at the side of the stage. Aisling was a little overexcited at becoming his assistant and told him that she couldn't wait to do the disappearing trick. Derek tried to smile, but all he could see was Suzi lying in her gore – a sight he would never forget.

Patty returned from her fans and asked Pete – who had apparently become her new minder – to take her to Tilly. She seemed upset as she approached, and Tilly took her somewhere quiet to talk. 'What's happened?' she asked. 'You look like you've seen a ghost.'

'More like smelt one,' said Patty, slumping down on a sofa. 'That perfume again. It was on one of the cats at the stage door: a round, grey, fat cat, done up like a throwback from the sixties. I'm sure I recognised her voice, although she didn't say much. I know it's impossible, but she could easily be the cat who knocked you down the steps.'

It wasn't the first time that Tilly had wanted to share the case with Patty, but she couldn't risk it: the less the punk star knew, the more likely she was to behave normally. She was pleased to know that Belisha Beacon was in the vicinity, though; Hettie's plan was on course. 'Well, we may never know who that was,' Tilly lied. 'I'm sure they're long gone with the tour money by now.'

'Ah, but you're wrong there, right? I didn't get a chance to say earlier, and it's a bit of a bad scene anyway, but I saw Deirdre get a load of notes out of her case and stuff them under Poppa's seat on the bus. I didn't know it was her at the time because I had no idea what she looked like, but as soon as I realised at breakfast, I couldn't decide what to do. With Suzi buggering off and Alice gone, I couldn't afford another band crisis, but I'm sure Poppa will be pleased to find his missing dosh.'

'I'd be *very* pleased,' said Poppa, catching the tail end of Patty's comment, 'but I doubt we'll see that sort of cash again. Are you ready for your soundcheck?'

Patty gave Tilly a knowing smile and the three cats headed for the stage. After making sure that Patty had everything she needed, Tilly left her tuning Suzi's bass and joined Hettie at the mixing desk, bursting to tell her about Deirdre's part in the missing money and share the even bigger news that Belisha Beacon had been sighted by Patty at the stage door.

'Game on, then!' said Hettie. 'I'm going to have a chat with Bruiser in the lighting box. Don't take your eyes off Derek or Aisling – we know they're both in danger. If you see Bondage Pete, get him to lock all the venue doors until gig time. We don't want any more surprises unless we're ready for them.'

Meanwhile, Belisha Beacon sat on a bench, stuffing her mouth with hot, greasy chips. She was really looking forward to the gig tonight – especially the final performance of Magical Mystery Paws.

Chapter Twenty-Six

Hettie called a meeting on the bus with Poppa, Bruiser, Marley, Tilly and Morbid, who'd returned from her sunbathing. She outlined her plan, giving everyone an important role, and when the business was concluded, Marley wheeled a high tea of tinned-salmon sandwiches and cake along the pier to the venue, having decided to keep her fish stew for supper, when she thought it would be more appreciated. Morale was greatly improved by her arrival, and a well-fed company began to look forward to the show.

The stage was set, the performers were ready and the queue to get in snaked along Lowerslop Pier. On Hettie's instructions, Bruiser walked the line, hoping to get an early sighting of Belisha, but the fans stretched ten cats across and it was impossible to spot anyone in particular. Bondage Pete threw the doors open at seven-thirty for a seven-forty-five start, and Aisling took up her position in Derek's magic box just before the audience was admitted. She knew she'd have to wait fifteen minutes before show time, so she took a Curly Wurly chocolate bar with her to pass the time. Derek paced at the side of the stage, waiting for Pete to announce him.

With so few of the tour party in on Hettie's plan, all the resources of the No. 2 Feline Detective Agency had to be put into action: Poppa was down in the audience with his mixing desk; Tilly was at the main fire exit door; Marley and Morbid were covering the other two exits; and Hettie and Bruiser were up in the lighting box with Flaky. At Hettie's request, Cormac had crept behind the drum kit, ready to offer a drum roll for dramatic effect as Derek opened the box, and Boobah had been told that if anything went wrong with Derek's act she should push the dancers onto the stage immediately.

As the audience filled the hall, Flaky projected a psychedelic bubble machine onto them, much to their delight; they laughed at each other's faces and paws, as the colour wash swept across them, and Bruiser and Hettie took the opportunity to observe the crowd, without Flaky having any idea who they were looking for. It was a standing-only show and the audience milled round, greeting friends and checking out the best vantage points for the stage. Bondage Pete had packed the cats in like sardines, allowing tickets to be oversold by at least fifty extra entries.

Hettie and Bruiser had no luck in sighting Belisha, but with seconds to go, Tilly waved her paw to attract Hettie's attention. She pointed to a clutch of cats close to the front, and Hettie snatched the bubble machine away from Flaky to train it on the spot that Tilly had indicated. 'Bingo!' she said, as the machine shot bubbles across Belisha Beacon's face. 'You can't get more brazen than that – right in front of the stage. Come on, Bruiser. Let's get this sorted.'

Bruiser and Hettie made a swift exit, leaving Flaky looking bewildered, as Bondage Pete walked out onto the stage. Flaky picked him up with the followspot, incorporating Derek's magic box, which twinkled as if it had just landed in a shower of stars. 'Welcome to another great gig here at Lowerslop Pier,' Pete said. 'Tonight we bring you one of the greatest punk rockers of our time, supported by Kitty O'Shea's dance troupe, all the way from Donegal. But first, the one and only Magical Mystery Paws!'

The audience was clearly there to see Patty Sniff, but decided to be generous. The fans gave Derek a warm welcome, clapping their paws and even stamping their feet, and Hettie and Bruiser were able to flank Belisha at a distance, without arousing her suspicions. Derek shaded his eyes from the spotlight now trained on him, and Hettie thought for a moment that he was going to freeze; as he picked the microphone out of its stand, she realised that it was part of his performance. 'Have any of you out there seen my glamorous assistant?' he shouted. A resounding 'no' came back to him from the audience. 'Well, she must be here somewhere,' Derek insisted.

'Look in the box!' shouted a long-haired black cat on the front row, who obviously wanted to be part of the show.

'Ah, you think she might be in my magic box, do you?'

'Yes!' screamed the audience.

'Then I'd better have a look.' Derek signalled to Cormac, who responded with a drum roll. The magician moved to the box and pulled it open with a flourish, revealing the pretty little Irish cat, who preened and wriggled as Derek offered her his paw. In an instant, Belisha sprang onto the stage, screeching and waving a long-bladed knife. She lunged at Derek before Bruiser could get to her, slashing his arm, and then turned on Aisling, who'd shot back into the box to protect herself. Bruiser made a grab for the knife as Hettie pulled Belisha to the ground, and the audience stood in silence while the drama played itself out.

Bondage Pete, who'd been watching from the wings, was horrified at the scene in front of him: Derek left a trail of blood as he exited the stage; Aisling crouched in the magic box, frightened to come out; and both Hettie and Bruiser were sitting on top of Belisha Beacon as she struggled and spat. It was the long-haired black cat on the front row who saved the day, shouting, 'Brilliant!' at the top of his voice and starting a round of applause. The clapping ran like a wave from the front to the back of the hall, and Hettie and Bruiser responded by dragging Belisha to her feet and forcing her into a bow before pulling her backstage. Aisling followed, adding a dainty curtsy, and Pete pushed a still-bleeding Derek back on to take a bow. With Boobah's encouragement, the Irish dancers bobbed on to a brisk set of jigs from Enya.

The audience was delighted with the opening to the concert. Most of them had seen the violence which punk concerts created in the early days, but this was a modern and truly innovative way to start a gig and they loved it – especially the slashing, which they found very realistic. Magical Mystery Paws was a hit for everyone, except the screaming banshee who Bruiser had just tied to a chair.

Tilly had been watching the pantomime unfold, and if she hadn't known the truth, she too would have given full marks to Derek and Belisha's performance: it was so well executed that it might have won an Oscar in Hollywood circles. She wanted to be there for the end of the story so she made her way round to the stage door and into the wings, where she could hear Belisha Beacon's muffled screams of protest. Tilly arrived to a very strange scene indeed: Derek was standing by the sink, wrapping a tea towel round his arm to stem the bleeding, while Belisha squirmed, trying to free herself from the chair she was tied to. She offered muted threats through the handkerchief that Hettie had forced into her mouth and, perhaps most bizarrely of all, Patty Sniff and Deirdre Nightshade stood by, dressed in full punk regalia, while Kitty O'Shea's dance troupe thundered and tapped their way through an amended version of Riverdance, this time without the water.

Belisha finally ran out of energy and sat limply in her chair. The realisation that she'd been thwarted in her mission of revenge was beginning to dawn on her. 'If you promise to stop screaming, I'll take the handkerchief away,' said Hettie. Belisha nodded and Bruiser stepped forward to remove the gag, fearing that she may bite in retaliation. She didn't, and just sat quietly. 'I honestly don't know what we're going to do with you,' Hettie continued, pulling a chair up to sit in front of her prisoner. 'I think it's time for some explanations.'

Belisha shot a look at Derek, and Bruiser moved forward, ready to replace the gag if necessary, but she spoke in almost a whisper. 'It's all 'is fault, makin' promises 'e couldn't keep, two-timin' me with that worthless drummer. She thought she could take me on, but I was too good for 'er. It took seconds to put 'er out of 'er misery. And then 'e kicks me off the tour, leavin' me stranded, and takes up with another of these punk sirens.' At this point, Belisha shot a look at Patty and Deirdre, before continuing. 'I'd encouraged 'im with 'is act. I'd even worked out the tricks for 'im, and what does 'e do? Drapes 'imself all over the Quake cat while she bathes in my glory. Yes, I watched through the window at Wobbleswick while they performed my tricks to that oh-so-bloody adoring audience. I bided me time and waited till I could get 'er on 'er own, and then I congratulated 'er on the saw trick and asked 'er to show me 'ow it was done. The magic box was by the bus and she stupidly lay in it. She looked shocked when I started to stab at 'er – a bit 'ere and a bit there, then I went in for the kill. It's a shame you found 'er before the show tonight. I was lookin' forward to seein' 'er again.'

Hettie had met some bad cats in her time as a detective, but until now she had always found something redeemable about them – or at least an understanding of why they'd done what they'd done; this time, as she looked at the miserable cat before her, she knew she was staring at the personification of evil. 'So why attack Patty?' she asked, keen to get the full story. 'She had nothing to do with Derek.'

'She got in my way,' Belisha replied. 'First at Tabby Road, in the café, where she treated me like a servant, puttin' on 'er "I'm a blind rock star" act. And then that night at Felix Toe. I wanted to trash the bus and there she was, lyin' on me bed in the back, so I watched 'er for a bit and then bashed 'er on the 'ead' – twice, I think. Anyway, I stuffed up there 'cause she didn't die, more's the pity. I could 'ave saved the planet from another 'as-been if I'd got that right. I did manage to trash the bus at Wobbleswick, though – a sort of celebration for stabbin' another Cheese Triangle. And what sort of a name is that?'

That was the first of Belisha's comments which Hettie had actually agreed with, but there was another pressing question which concerned them all. 'And what about the tour money you stole?'

Belisha looked indignant for the first time and responded with a denial. 'What money? I didn't steal no money. You can't pin that on me.'

Tilly tried to attract Hettie's attention, as Deirdre shuffled from one Doc Marten to another, and Patty threw a knowing glance in Tilly's direction. There had been no time to update Hettie or Poppa on the missing money, and Tilly had quite forgotten to look under Poppa's seat when they'd had the meeting on the bus earlier. Belisha sensed some confusion in her captors and took the opportunity to loosen the string that Bruiser had used to tie her paws behind her back. Loud applause was coming from the stage, which meant that the Irish dancers would be backstage at any minute, and Belisha hoped that the distraction would give her time to escape.

Bruiser excused himself to go and reset the stage with Poppa, ready for Patty's gig, and the wings were suddenly filled with hot, out of breath, triumphant dancers, all pleased that their performance had gone down so well. In her excitement, Boobah managed to get her wheelchair stuck in the doorway, and it was while everyone was pulling and tugging at it that Belisha made her bid for freedom. Ripping the fur from her paws, she struggled free and took a mighty leap over Boobah's head. She ran on through the doorway, crossing the stage like a whirlwind, and then bounded out onto the pier, heading back towards the town – and freedom. Hettie, Tilly, Bruiser and Poppa gave chase, as Belisha scattered startled cats like ninepins along the pier in the late evening sunshine – and if it hadn't been for the Promenade Tram Company, she would have got clean away.

There was no time for the tram driver to apply his brakes, as the hurtling ball of grey fluff bounded off the pier and straight into his path. Hettie, Tilly, Poppa and Bruiser cannoned into each other, bringing the chase to an end, and the tram driver left his vehicle to inspect the scene. Belisha Beacon's body was scattered along the rails like a doll which a petulant kitten had torn apart.

Chapter Twenty-Seven

Looking back, there would be some good memories of the Summer of Fluff Tour, which Hettie and Tilly would remind each other of from time to time. Alice and Suzi would be remembered with the affection afforded to those who die young. Hettie's brief return to music would stand out as a personal triumph. Then there was Tilly's continuing friendship with Patty Sniff, who regularly dropped in to visit whenever she passed through the town, often escorted by Bondage Pete, who'd become the love of her life. It was curious that Patty only shared the miracle of getting her sight back with a few close friends, as if more than happy to continue to hide behind her dark glasses. After the tour, her *Sausage and Slash* album topped the charts for sixteen weeks in a row, making it the fastest-selling punk album of all time. Deirdre Nightshade – who'd owned up to stealing the tour money and had been forgiven – was making a good living as a session guitarist at Tabby Road. Kitty O'Shea's Irish dance troupe secured a lucrative residency on TV's *Strictly Come Prancing*, and Boobah went on to win gold at the Feline Paralympics, coming first in the 400-metre wheelchair dash. Perhaps the most heart-warming story of all concerned Psycho Derek: his wish to be an artist was finally granted when Patty employed him to design all her future album covers; with her patronage, the music industry was begging for his artwork.

Several months after the tour, Poppa paid a call on Hettie and Tilly, wearing the widest grin that any cat could muster.

'Whatever's happened?' Hettie asked. 'I hope you're not planning another bloody tour, because if you are, we're busy.'

Poppa reduced his grin to a smile and unwrapped a parcel he'd been carrying, putting it down on the table.

'Ooh, look!' said Tilly. 'It's Patty's new album!'

Hettie stared at the mass of faces on the colourful front cover, realising that they were all familiar to her. There was Tilly, Poppa, Bruiser, Marley, Flaky, Deirdre, Boobah, all the Irish dancers, Bondage Pete, Suzi Quake, Alice Slap and a prominent picture of Hettie herself. The front of the album was entirely dedicated to the Summer of Fluff Tour, beautifully painted by Psycho Derek, but it was the album's title that Hettie loved most.

'*Sgt Poppa's Lonely Hearts Club Band*,' she said. 'Nice one!'

Author's Note and Acknowledgements

I have always been a Beatles fan and it's no real surprise that I would eventually offer a playful nod to them and the world they inhabited. My own music touring days were very much an inspiration for this book, and it was a joy to recreate some of the characters I met along the way – adding whiskers and tails on this particular journey. I've also borrowed names from some of my favourite Irish musicians, who have had a profound effect on my life and work as a journalist.

I would like to thank Pete Duncan for believing in the series, my editor Abbie Headon for pawing over the manuscript and laughing in all the right places, designer Jason Anscomb for being our resident Psycho Derek, my readers for their continuing enthusiasm for Hettie and Tilly's world, and Nicola for her love and support always. I hope all your summers are full of fluff!

About the Author

Mandy Morton was born in Suffolk and after a short and successful music career in the 1970s as a singer-songwriter – during which time she recorded six albums and toured extensively throughout the UK and Scandinavia with her band – she joined the BBC, where she produced and presented arts-based programmes for local and national radio. She more recently presents The Eclectic Light Show on Cambridge 105 Radio. Mandy lives with her partner, who is also a crime writer, in Cambridge and Cornwall where there is always room for a long-haired tabby cat. She is the author of The No. 2 Feline Detective Agency series and also co-wrote *In Good Company* with Nicola Upson, which chronicles a year in the life of The Cambridge Arts Theatre.

Twitter: **@hettiebagshot and @icloudmandy**

Facebook: **HettieBagshotMysteries**

Preview

COMING SOON

The Moving Claw
(The No. 2 Feline Detective Agency)

The town's psychic cat, Irene Peggledrip, is being visited by a band of malevolent spirits who all claim to be murderers. The stage is set for Hettie and Tilly to solve an old murder mystery, where all the cats involved appear to be dead.

Will all the ghosts come home to roost?

And who is stealing the cheese from the mouse trap?

Join Hettie and Tilly for another spirited adventure!

Note from the Publisher

To receive updates on new releases in The No. 2
Feline Detective Agency series – plus special offers
and news of other humorous fiction series to make
you smile – sign up now to the Farrago mailing list at
farragobooks.com/sign-up